POPCORN & GUTS

SCARY STORIES

First paperback edition 2025
Published by Silver Bullet Books
450 Jack Sharp Dr.
Seymour, TN 37865
For information email:
tuckerjoneson@gmail.com
Cover Design by Tucker Joneson

Paperback ISBN: 979-8-9921655-2-4
Ebook ISBN: 979-8-9921655-3-1

CONTENTS

For Papa, our Wolfman…

INTRODUCTION

After writing my first horror book, *Blood in the Dark: Thirteen Tales of Terror*, I knew I couldn't stop. I needed to write more, so here we are! Writing this second collection of short stories was even more fun than the first—and now feeling a little more like I knew what I was doing this time—it flew by. Some of these stories I had written years ago, and were nearly added to my first book, while others I came up with as I was putting this second book together.

If you enjoyed my werewolf stories in the first book, there's another in here for you! Ghosts will once more haunt you, and new types of aliens will attack. Rotting clowns, mummy curses and so much more await you in the shadows. Nowhere in this book are you safe from frights! If you—like me—are ecstatic when diving into the world of the supernatural and love the feeling of goosebumps crawling up your spine, then you'll get a kick out of the gruesome tales beyond this page! Enjoy!

POPCORN & GUTS

Busy like a hive, dozens of frantic shoppers scampered along the busy mall food court. A slender boy with spindly limbs and curly dark hair sat alone lumped over his lunch. After taking the last few bites of his greasy slice of pepperoni pizza, he slurped down his fizzy soda and smeared a crumpled napkin across his face. The seventeen-year-old, once thrilled for summer break, was now regretting his first summer job. Not wanting to check the time, he reluctantly raised his wrist watch up over his plate.

Two more minutes. Woo-hoo. He somberly thought. *These lunch breaks never last...*

The young movie theater employee let out an exhausted sigh and slowly rose from the table. Bill begrudgingly adjusted his name tag and made his way through the crowded mall. It was the Fourth of July and business was booming. Big and small, every shop and business inside the Westhill Mall was having their own holiday sale—even the movie theater. Everything at the concession stand was half-off and the crowds came rolling in. The endless waves of sweaty shoppers crowding the cramped theater lobby reminded him of a zombie apocalypse. The only thing worse than surviving the end of the world—was working it.

The employee slunk his way past the mess of people in line. An exhausted mother stood over her energetic child, eager for a taste of the coveted candies behind the glass counter. A high school couple stood behind them. The boy in the jersey had his arm around his girl, slowly sliding his hand down into her left butt pocket. The bubbly girlfriend chewed her gum and twirled her curly hair as her eyes looked lost in the menu that hung over the cashier. He could smell her sweet cherry perfume as he walked past them, before turning the corner and picking up the broom and dustpan that were stored in the maintenance closet.

The film in theater four was just ending as dozens of people came stumbling through the door. Bill nodded and forced a smile as the audience members passed him by. There was a blazing heat outside—and even with the reinforced air-conditioner units that cooled the entirety of the large mall—some of those people walking past Bill still smelled like they had run a marathon through an outhouse while they sat inside that theater. After desperately spitting the taste of sweat and butter out of his mouth, Bill made his way inside.

The credits rolled on as the intense synth-soundtrack blared through the speakers. Bill chuckled when he saw the title, "Black Friday 5: Seasons Beatings" scroll across the screen.

"Another slasher sequel…" He muttered to himself while he swept up crumbs and wrappers that littered the aisles.

How many more times can that killer come back from the grave?!

A moment later and the studio logo came to life, filling the room with that familiar company jingle. Bill thought the room was empty, as his eyes were still re-adjusting to the darkness, until he spotted movement in the back corner of the theater. He stepped further up the stairs towards the mysterious figure. Digging through his pockets, he finally retrieved his flashlight, shining it ahead of him.

"Hey, knock it off!" He ordered. "Movie's over. Get out of here!"

The young couple retrieved their tongues from their throats and awkwardly rose to their feet. They grabbed their half-empty popcorn bucket and shuffled down the aisle. Even in the dark, Bill could see the embarrassed girlfriend blushing as she adjusted her tight shirt.

Popcorn better be the only mess they left behind.

As he continued sweeping up bits of popcorn and candy wrappers in the now silent rows of seats, he looked around and noticed something off. It was still dark inside the theater.

The lights should have turned on by now. He thought, glancing up at the dusty ceiling.

"Hey, Sarah! Turn on the lights! Quit messing with me!"

There was no answer. Standing there, alone in the quiet black room, reminded him of all the stories he'd been told. With a shrug, he would scoff at his coworkers who told tales of the ghosts that supposedly haunted this theater. They would spend quiet nights when no customers were around debating the spirits' origins.

Who were they? Why were they here? What did they want?

Bill didn't care.

He thought—no, he knew—that all of that was a bunch of nonsense. Flickering lights and a chill in the air would get the others giddy, while it just made him roll his eyes. Sarah, the goth chick that gave most kids the creeps, would say that it was the spirit of a construction worker. She claimed that he fell to his death from the top floor of the three story structure while welding support beams together. Bill's co-workers believed that the construction worker's body was entombed in the concrete foundations of the structure, while his spirit haunts the grounds to this day.

What a bunch of Bull. Was all that he had to say to that.

Another coworker, Melvin—a neurotic little dweeb that was barely old enough to work there— would claim that the mall was constructed over some kind of ancient burial grounds. Bill couldn't remember all of the other tall tales they would spread. All he knew was that it was a big waste of time. They just liked to pass the time sharing stories and seeing who could out-spook the others. The theater was made cheap and the wiring was faulty. Nothing more. After only working there for two months, he had seen enough. For the first time in his life, Bill was actually excited for summer to be over and looked forward to the fall.

Stepping out from the shadows of the movie room, and back into the bright lobby, he was greeted by the roars of the holiday crowds. Customers overflowed the queue leading up to the snack stand. Popcorn butter ran down the edge of the mustard-stained counter while crumpled candy wrappers littered the carpet around the trash can. With a subtle shake of his head, he asked himself, "How hard is it for people to throw their trash away?"

Before he could kneel down to clean up the mess, he spotted something in the corner of his eye. Two young boys were sneaking around the crowded line in the lobby and headed for a theater.

"Hey, you two!" Bill called out. He quickly skipped ahead and cut them off near the concession stand. "Where are your tickets, kids? …And where are your parents?"

"We're thirteen!" The one boy shouted. He had wavy blonde hair and the other boy's head was buzzed. The blonde wore a metal band shirt with faded jeans and the other in a bright blue skater tank top. They looked just like the type of twerps to break windows with rocks and ding-dong-ditch his neighborhood. Bill was not in the mood to deal with these kids today.

"Fat chance. You guys look like you're barely eleven." Bill argued, noticing the gaps from missing teeth when the blonde kid spoke.

"Screw you!" The other boy sneered.

"Wow…Even if you had tickets, I have the ability to kick you out of here." His grimace turned to a smile, "…Which is exactly what I'm going to do!"

"Hey, over here!' An overweight lady snapped her fingers at the theater attendant. "Look at this line, kid! We need to get to our movie!" He ignored the older woman in the ugly brown pant suit that was two sizes-too small for her large frame. Her heavy makeup only enhanced her miserable scowl. The theater worker's fuse was running short as he irritably shooed the children towards the exit.

"What a dickwad!" The blonde boy muttered.

Before he could scold the brats, he heard someone shout his name. Turning around, he spotted his supervisor calling for him, and like a dog for a treat, Bill scampered over to him. The older man's thinning hair clung to his sweaty scalp. He shuffled back and forth retrieving popcorn for customers as they handed over crumpled cash. There was only one other employee working that day, and she was on her lunch break. The others called out sick, leaving this skeleton crew drowning in the sea of shoppers. Before Bill could even force a smile, the old man barked from behind the cash register.

"Billy, go check on the projector in theater six!" He said, wiping sweat from his brow that more than likely dripped down into the bucket of popcorn he was holding. "A customer said it wasn't working right. The movie's about to start, so get going!"

Bill nodded and quickly walked back to the maintenance closet. He tossed the broom inside and swung the door shut behind him. Theater six was located at the end of the hallway. Passing theater two, he heard the sound of explosions and gunfire from the latest action blockbuster. While theater three played a preview for a new animated princess film coming out later that month. For just a moment, the magic of the movies carried his mind far away from the chaos of the crowds and the boiling temperatures outside. He took in the aroma of hot dogs and candy in the air as he heard people cheering and laughing in the rooms around him.

Bill loved movies and the way they could take you away with them to other worlds, both exciting and terrifying, for just a couple of hours before returning to reality. The walls of his room at home were covered in film posters, and his love for the medium is what drove him to start this summer job. It wasn't all bad. He had his good days, but some of these people really tested him—and his boss wasn't the most pleasant man to work with, either. Bill just couldn't wait for the summer crowds to die down. It had been steadily busy the last three weeks, always keeping him on his toes from clock in to closing, and today was twice as bad.

Only four more hours...

The thought of stripping off his uniform and driving his beat-up red Volkswagen home brought him right back to reality. The smell of sweets faded—as did his smile. He reached his hand out and pulled the door to theater six open. A new smell overcame his senses. Something unusual.

Something was burning!

Bill turned around and ran for their employee door. In a flash, he passed through the hall and was nearing the projector room. Beams of bright light flickered through the gap under the door, reaching out to him like frantic pale fingers. He clasped his fist around the oddly warm metal handle and yanked the door open. The small projector room was in complete disarray. Bill thought it looked like they were robbed or that a tornado had blown through the building. Several heavy metal film containers were spilled open with the reels strung along the dirty floor. Strips of film hung from half-open cabinet doors. Paperwork and forms were scattered along the ground while their tool boxes were tossed across the room, leaving an explosion of equipment throughout the space. The large movie projector standing before him had still been running. Loose film frantically flapped in a loop as it continued to malfunction. The sound cracked like a whip and it only grew louder and faster.

What the hell is going on here?

Puzzled, he cautiously walked into the chaotic, cramped room. Watching his step, he maneuvered around the scattered items and film strips that crawled along the floor like curly fingers. It was overwhelmingly hot in the room. He noticed the heat was radiating from the projector. It felt like reaching into an oven as he extended his fingers out towards the machine. The moment his finger touched the glowing power switch, a bolt of energy surging from the projector passed through his arm like lightning. An explosion of electricity shot through his nervous system. His feet were locked in place. His teeth ached as they were tightly clenched and his limbs began frantically shaking. He had no control. A few milliseconds felt like several agonizing minutes. All he could do was stand there and ride out the pain. A moment later and everything went black. Bill was gone.

––––––––

Everything hurt. His ears rang as his vision was blurry and his swollen eyes watered. He stretched his legs, only for them to lock up. Bill hissed as his skin ached and cracked worse than any sunburn he ever had. The room was warm and damp. It was dark, but he knew that he was somewhere else. He wasn't in the movie theater anymore. Whatever he laid in was moist. It was slick and greasy like oil in a mechanic's garage. The smell of metal and gasoline coated the thick air as Billy struggled to take a breath. His vision finally came into focus as he slowly sat up from the dirty concrete floor. Rubbing his eyes, he unknowingly smeared the filth from his hands onto his face.

Blinking, the boy realized that he was in some kind of parking garage. He knew that he hadn't been to this place before, yet something about it all felt so familiar. Before he could figure it out, came the rush of another smell. Something awful—like an old diaper cooking in the sun. He wanted to gag. Keeping his composer, Bill focused on rising to his feet. The tingling pain continued to pass through his muscles. He pressed his right leg forward and started to rise. Wobbling, he quickly pushed his left foot out, and forced himself up. Like vicious claws, the aching agony clenched down onto his weak limbs, but the boy stood firm. He bit his tongue and stepped forward, ignoring the pain before it slowly faded away.

This has to be a dream.

Reaching out with his aching hands, he cautiously stepped towards the wall. His fingers passed over faded paint chipping away from the smooth stone walls until he finally felt the rigid framing of a door. Then he grasped the cold metal of the door handle and pulled it open. Instantly, he was greeted by a gust of dusty wind. The debris slid down his throat, stirring up gnarly coughs from the teenager. He squinted his eyes, struggling to see ahead of him. It was night time. A blur of light shown overhead, obstructed by clouds and dust. The crescent moon was alone with no sign of stars in sight. That's when he realized that it was much darker out than usual that night. That was, if he was even in California anymore. Wherever he was, it looked like a wasteland. Burnt out husks of cars littered the roads. Buildings stood dark and empty, crumbling in on themselves, like tombstones amongst the overgrown weeds. A world was falling apart under the relentless winds of a disastrous dust storm. What he couldn't see—were people.

"Hello?" He nervously called out. "Anyone out ther—"

Bill stopped himself when he heard something shifting to his right. It was a dark blur as it passed a row of glass doors, with one swinging open. Was it just from the gust of wind or was someone really there? He watched for any movement, besides the slowly closing creaking door, but there was nothing more. The door finally clicked shut, sealing the entrance to a massive structure that stood across the road from him, looming over Bill like a great white in dark waters. Biting his tongue, he debated following the mysterious noise—unsure of the danger that could be awaiting him.

Better than just sitting here in this dank place. He told himself, unsure if he believed it.

Once again, he wasn't sure what the large building was that resided before him, but there was something about it that seemed oddly familiar. Moonlight gleamed off the ridges of the dark door frames ahead. They remained closed, yet he felt the sense of them welcoming him in. Stepping outside of the humid garage, he checked his surroundings once more before pressing onward into the dark, decrepit structure. The air was stale and thick with the scent of human waste and copper. Nearly blinded by the nothingness of his surroundings, he shambled forward spotting something flickering off in the distance. A single warm glow was the only sign of life in this endless black abyss. It was a fire—lit in an old metal trash can. Cautiously warming his hands, Bill noticed something illuminated by the fire. It was a warning. Bold letters written with neon green spray-paint were plastered across the pale wall.

STOP THE MIND-MITES!
Mind-Mites…Where have I heard that before?

His eyes continued to travel down the wall only to discover something piled in the corner, just out of reach of the fire's light. It wasn't furniture or trash. It was a body. The blood-soaked body of an older man slumped over a metal bench. This man appeared homeless, hidden under baggy, shredded clothes. A shopping cart filled with random items was left on its side to his right. Bill swallowed a lump in his throat, trying his best not to throw up. He harshly exhaled, desperate to avoid the putrid fumes of the rotting corpse.

Nervously kneeling down closer to the body, he discovered the dark blood that pooled around it was dry and sticky. He spotted a small metal flashlight next to the old man's leg and reached for it. Clicking the switch, it activated a bright beam that cut through the shadows around him. Bill turned the light back towards the body, but even under the thick beard and messy hair, he didn't recognize the stranger. Gently pushing the man's shoulder forward, he rolled him onto his stomach, where he was met with a disgusting discovery.

Bill gasped, stumbling back in horror. The back of the old man's skull and neck that were torn open and eaten away at. Under his scraggly gray hair were large bloody incisions. A long cavity ran down his flesh from the back of his skull to the top of his shoulders. Lingering inside this canyon of gore was a glowing violet substance. The substance—which appeared thick like blood—was shining bright from within the dark ditch of the corpse.

"Oh my God!" Bill screamed, scrambling back and losing his balance. He crashed back against the wall, eyes still locked on the body on the ground. The purple carnage seemed to glow brighter the longer he looked at it. Finally, Bill shut his eyes and caught his breath. He knew where he was. He didn't know how this was happening, but he knew what was going on. It was insane. He thought he was going crazy. He couldn't bring himself to say it out loud. It was impossible—but here he was.

I'm in a movie! I'm in that zombie-alien-thing movie, "End of Days!"

Bill's mind rattled as he looked at his surroundings. He recognized the filming locations. He recognized the writing on the wall. Then he looked back down at the purple slime oozing out of the back of the homeless man's skull.

"This has to be a prank or something…" He muttered. "This isn't possible!"

He remembered watching the movie one night after work in his theater. It had just come out a few weeks ago. He thought of the monsters—alien bugs from another world that arrived here inside a meteor. Only a few at first, rapidly multiplied into hundreds of thousands and eventually billions, taking over the world. That's when he stopped in his tracks. He realized how the movie ended. It was a tragedy—ending with everyone dying. There was no escape. No surviving this apocalypse. They were screwed. He was screwed.

Crawling around the corner, Bill realized just where he was. He was in the middle of the mall in the fictional town of Santa Toro. He was surrounded by the shops and restaurants he recognized as the key locations of the film.

"There's the candy shop! And the busted elevator…So the camping store they ran to in the movie should be right around that corner!" He gleamed, beginning to recognize the layout of the mall. For just a moment, he felt hope in this living nightmare.

Before he could fully wrap his mind around the world he was thrown into, he spotted someone standing by the fountain ahead. Water limply trickled from top of the cracked sculpture. The dark figure lifelessly teetered in the breeze. A dirty, ragged coat covered a slender man underneath it. The stranger was hunched over with dark, scraggly hair covering his face. Knowing something was wrong, Bill stayed hidden, turning off his flashlight and crouching behind a burnt-out pretzel stand.

"Please! Help me!" A scream rang out across the mall. He cautiously stayed down, unsure of who to trust. Keeping his head on a swivel, he searched for the woman in distress. "I saw you in the alley! Please! I—"

He slowly peaked over the counter, the smell of stale bread and ash lingered under his nose. Across the wide open space of the mall, he spotted movement. A middle-aged woman hung from the ledge of the third floor above, with another figure looming over her. Her legs kicked frantically as she held on. A zombie-like body reached down for her as she screamed. As the body bent over, Bill witnessed a giant insect clasped onto the back of the figure's neck. The alien's wings twitched as it pulled its head loose from the bleeding gap of the corpse's spine.

"Mind-mites…"

The creature was made up of shades of blues and greens with black spots like one of those poisonous frogs found in the Amazon. It had a dozen spindly legs protruding from its core that wrapped around the corpse it was controlling. Prickly hairs and spikes ran along the dark legs that looked sharp enough to slice the zombie's throat open with ease. The alien's antennas twitched and changed directions like they were searching for a signal. A thick mucus dripped down from within the creature's shadowy underbelly.

Watching this thing churned Bill's stomach. Finally looking away, almost feeling entranced by the monster, he searched for a way up to the woman on the third floor. At the other end of the large hall ahead of him were the escalators. Not in operation, they were burnt from engine fires and the steps were covered with furniture and other miscellaneous objects. Whoever was hiding out in the mall attempted to block the zombies from coming up to the higher floors.

Looks like that didn't work out.

The woman cried out in terror as the zombie grabbed her wrist and effortlessly lifted her up to his eye level. Desperate, she swung her other arm at the stranger, beating him with any energy she had left.

The figure didn't flinch as it brought her closer to him. The alien bug crawled over the zombies's shoulder and climbed onto the woman. She cried and cursed, shaking her head like a mad woman. The alien paid no attention as it inspected her spine. Bill sat there helplessly hunched behind the car. He was frozen. Unable to do anything, but watch as this monster attacked. It quickly lunged its head forward, biting down into her flesh. It tore back at her skin, slicing her open. Blood dripped down the building as the creature began to take over his new host.

With one last desperate strike, she swung her legs, kicking the corpse in the stomach and launching herself away from the ledge. The rotting body lost its grip on the woman and she was sent soaring through the air. The alien still had its face buried into her neck as they fell towards the Earth. In her final moments she grabbed hold of the insect, not allowing it to fly away. Seconds later Bill heard a loud splat like a gunshot ringing across the land. Blood and alien slimed oozed and pooled along the bottom floor of the mall. Another body in a sea of carnage.

Other zombie figures came limping out from shops and staggered across the bottom floor ahead. They curiously surrounded the woman's body, ignoring their fallen soldier. The aliens on their backs bit deeper into their necks before the zombies dropped to the floor and began tearing the woman's corpse apart. The insects hissed like cicadas in unison as they consumed her flesh.

Trembling as he looked over his shoulder, Bill spotted a flickering neon sign hanging loosely from the wall, looming over the dark entrance of a department store. A rolling metal gate hung partially open over the abandoned storefront. He took a breath, and a somewhat sigh of relief, slowing his rapidly beating heart. With no other options, he tiptoed towards the storefront.

Swiftly slipping through the opening and into the dark void of the business, he was greeted with the smell of rot. Then came the groans of corpses. He wasn't alone. Dozens of drooling figures mumbled incoherent words and squealed as they shuffled through the large, empty department store. Mannequins stood scattered across the dimly-lit floor of the store. The shadows intermixing with the twitching possessed bodies. Billy could hear the wings of the alien insects flutter and fidget in the dark. His skin crawled as he imagined one of those things crawling up his back and biting down into his neck. Their long mandibles were slick and deadly like daggers. For once, the movie cameras didn't exaggerate—they looked even bigger in person!

How did this even happen?! Why am I here?!

Bill tore at his hair, crouched down against the dusty shop counter. The ground was sticky and covered in mold. Any other day he would be disgusted, but today mold was the least of his worries. The wooden counter creaked behind him. The frightened kid held his breath, as the corpse of a woman groaned just over his head. The woman's eyes were a faded white like sour milk, floating in the dark pits of her sockets. Red messy hair clung to the corpse's pale skin. It dragged its broken limb across the counter while the alien twitched on its back.

His beating heart thumped in his skull as his lungs burned for air. Seconds passed like minutes before the woman finally turned and limped away, back into the shadows. Taking a deep breath, the boy clenched his teeth and quickly crawled across the tile floor. He rolled and backed up against an old cracked support beam, barely avoiding the sightline of an alien shambling towards him. Keeping his eyes locked on the figure around the corner, he slowly climbed to his feet.

Bill felt something warm on the back of his neck. Then came the sound of a corpse groaning behind him. Before he could turn around to face it, the rotting body tackled him, sending him crashing forward into the pillar. When the boy pressed up against the brittle column, he was met with a loud snapping sound. Instantaneously growing, the cracks spread across the concrete until reaching the ceiling. Rumblings traveled across the store, sprinkling debris and dust onto their shoulders as ceiling panels began to give out. Aggravated by the noises, the monsters squealed and spasmed throughout the dark business. The aliens twitched on their backs as the figures all suddenly shifted and turned facing towards Bill. He was surrounded.

"Oh God…"

Without a second thought, Bill ran. Bodies hissed and shrieked as they charged after the boy. Aliens crashed through coat hangers and store displays, hungry for another flesh bag. His lungs burned like fire as he leapt over counters and piles of knocked over clothes. He could see another open doorway just ahead.

Almost there!

A boney hand clasped down onto the boy's arm. He growled in pain as the jagged fingernails began to cut through his skin. He kept running, yanking his right arm forward, desperate to lose the monster. The husk of a body howled with breath that tasted like rotten apples in a gutter. He wanted to hurl, but kept his focus on his feet. He couldn't risk tripping with those things hot on his tail. Another boom crashed through the ceiling above him. Chunks of the wall imploded towards him. He used his free arm to shield his face, still pulling the body behind him. He looked over his shoulder again to see the body grow limp. In an instant it rushed towards the ground, face planting with a harsh thud and a crack before erupting like a rotten melon filled with blood. Still hovering in the air was the alien bug, now flying right at Bill's face. He screamed and swung his arm at it, still keeping an eye on the doorway ahead of him. Only a few feet away. Blindly, he kept swinging his arm back. He felt the brush of a wing graze his arm. It was warm and damp like a soggy towel. Again, he wanted to hurl.

One more violent swing of his arm and he made contact with the creature. It cried as his knuckles crushed the bug's face. He never looked back, but he imagined it was sent crashing into the wall. Its many legs and large wings twitching in the corner before the building put it out of its misery.

Another chunk of the ceiling came crashing down to his left. Coughing through the dust, he pushed even harder, until finally launching himself through the air and crash landing outside of the store.

Like rolling thunder, the department store collapsed in an explosion of dust and debris. Dodging the destruction by only inches, Bill made it out safely, while dozens of the decomposed attackers were crushed once and for all. Almost choking as he struggled to breathe through the bitter dust, he started laughing at his lucky survival. For just a moment, he felt hope in the middle of this living nightmare. Resting as the dust settled around him, he raised his head to look around. Whispers softly grew in the distance. The noises soon grew louder and appeared to multiply. Those whispers quickly turned to moans as Bill spotted figures shifting in the shadows.

Oh no…not more of them! He prayed.

Dozens of the undead-bodies shambled towards the boy. Their limbs twitched and jittered in inhuman ways. Their bloody fingers cracked as they reached out towards him. Bill skipped to his feet and ran. Unsure of where he was going, he didn't stop moving. Sweat ran down his face, burning as it dripped into his eye. Slamming into a wall, he sharply turned left down a hallway. Frantically searching his pockets and feeling nothing but lint, he came to the realization that he lost his flashlight. His burning eyes darted, searching for any sign of hope around him. The world was dark and growing darker as a storm came overhead. The beasts were still on his tail. The hissing of the alien insects, and the moans from the decomposing bodies they possessed, rattled the boy's bones and sent his shaking heart sinking to his stomach. There was no escape from this. There were too many of these things. He had nowhere to run. Nowhere to hide. This time he wouldn't live to see the credits roll.

Cheers erupted throughout the theater. Movie-goers laughed and tossed popcorn as others bunched up and screamed. Couples kissed in the dark corners of the room, ignorant of anything going on in the film. Sitting down at the front of the theater were the two young boys. The same ones that Bill tried to toss out earlier. For them, it was forty minutes ago, but for Bill it felt like a lifetime ago. With the grouchy theater worker out of the way, they snuck their way back inside. The two boys chuckled as they tossed popcorn down their throats. They watched with excitement as the frightened teen was chased down dark hallways by the brain-dead corpses, eager to tear him apart. Purple glowing slime dripped from their empty gaping mouths. Dark, lifeless eyes followed.

The blonde kid smiled, "This is the best movie I've seen all year!"

THE MUMMY'S FINGER

Cobwebs clung to Daryl's hair as he shifted boxes in the dingy basement. The dim light bulb flickered, barely illuminating the cold space. Some of the flimsy cardboard boxes were filled with photo albums and family memories, while others contained bizarre relics and oddities. Bugs displayed in glass frames and jars with dead plants. After piling several boxes at the bottom of the stairs, he turned his attention to an old rickety cabinet against the back wall of the basement. It looked older than his grandparents, which meant it was heavy, and that meant it would be a nightmare to push up the stairs.

Cracking his back with a stretch, he stepped over and took hold of the large, creaking cabinet, sliding it away from the wall. The boards of the dresser were all loose, just waiting to fall apart after years of collecting dust in the dank room. As he pushed the cabinet towards the stairs, he looked back over his shoulder and noticed something strange. A fresh wooden board appeared to be drilled into the brick wall.

"Holy smokes!" He whispered, pulling back at the loose corner of the wooden board. A small room was hidden behind it. Spotting something large lurking in the shadows, Daryl retrieved his phone, flipping on the flashlight. The bright beam revealed a large wooden crate sitting at the center of the dark, and otherwise empty, room. Years of dust had coated the secret shipping container.

Without hesitation, the man ran upstairs in search of his crowbar. A cautious voice in his head whispered of the worries he had, but he ignored it. He had to know what was in this crate.

Why would the owner board up this little room? All just for a single box?

———

"What's that, honey?" His wife asked from the top of the stairs, grocery bags still hung from her slender fingers. Jamie Frazer's short, curly hair twirled around her curious hazel eyes. Descending the steps, she inspected the large crate her husband was dragging along the floor.

"Not sure yet! I just found it!" He answered, excited by the discovery. "It was sitting in this secret room, hidden behind that old cabinet."

Her eyes followed his finger that pointed to the slim opening in the wall.

"Oh, wow! How weird!"

"Yeah, I'm thinking whatever is inside this crate must be valuable!" Daryl licked his lip as he pressed the crowbar under the lid.

"Let's hope so." She bit at her nail, watching the crowbar busting the lid loose. With one final push

—the crate burst open. The couple peered inside, shocked to discover such a small, strange thing sitting alone in the center of the massive box.

"What the hell is that?" Jamie asked.

"It's…a finger." He muttered, unable to take his eyes off of it. "It looks so old…" As he reached forward to pick it up, a chill ran up his spine. Daryl pulled his hand back. He could have sworn he almost heard a voice whisper in his ear.

"Grab me some medical gloves or something." He asked, turning back to his wife. "I'm no historian, but I know we shouldn't touch this with our bare hands."

"We shouldn't touch it at all!" She interjected.

"It's okay, baby. This guy left all kinds of weird stuff down here. Dead bugs in jars, stuffed birds, old documents and notebooks filled with scribbles." Daryl explained, pointing back at the stack of boxes resting at the bottom of the stairs. "He must have been some kind of scientist or history expert. Who knows, this house could have been owned by Indiana Jones!"

"Doesn't make it any less gross." She sighed.

"We need some extra cash, honey. We've put everything we have into this house. This could be a major win!" He smiled, rubbing her arm. He could see in her eyes that she was thinking it over, but still remained hesitant.

"You love all those graphic serial killer documentaries, but you can't handle a little mummy finger?" Daryl chuckled.

With a smirk, she gently smacked the back of her husband's head. "I'll go look for some gloves."

————

"Hey, Greg! Gotta ask you something, you got a minute?" Daryl called out, stepping out front of his house. The middle-aged, balding neighbor smiled under his bushy mustache as he walked back from checking his mailbox.

"Sure thing, what's up?" Greg answered, stepping over to Daryl's driveway. He glanced down, noticing a dirty rag in Daryl's hand. "What's that you're holding?"

Daryl unraveled the finger from the old cloth. The odd smell continued to radiate from the dried flesh.

"Jeez! What is that, Daryl?" Greg gasped.

"Some kind of mummified finger. It was in an old wooden crate hidden in our basement!"

"Seriously?"

"Can't make this stuff up!" Daryl shook his head with a grin, "…Along with lots of other odd things the past owner left behind."

Greg cautiously reached forward to pick up the dusty, white finger and take a closer look at it. Just as he clasped it between his fingers, Daryl pulled back.

"Hey, careful." Daryl warned. "Might not want the oils in our hand to damage it or anything, ya know?"

"Oh yeah, of course! Sorry!" Greg pulled his hand back, rubbing it nervously.

As they looked it over, a middle-school boy rode his skateboard down the sidewalk. Skidding to a stop, his scruffy blonde hair bounced under his helmet as he stepped over to the two men.

"Woah, what is that?"

"Hey, Scottie. Well, I'm not exactly sure yet. Some kind of mummy finger, I believe." Daryl said, holding it closer to the kid. "The old owner was some kind of scientist. He had all kinds of strange things he left in the basement."

The boy's eyes grew wide in wonder. "Sick!"

"Did you guys know him well?" Daryl asked them. "You know what he was into? What he was studying before he passed?"

"No. Not really." Greg sighed, "He never really came out much. Stayed to himself. Focused on his studies, I guess."

"Yeah. I think I only ever saw him, like twice. Kind of creeped me out." Scottie added, kicking up his skateboard.

"Hmm…" Daryl nodded, "I'll need to find some kind of expert to show this to. See if it's worth anything."

"I got a buddy that works at the Natural History Museum, downtown." Greg tapped Daryl's arm. "I don't know if this is really his area of expertise, but he may be able to help!"

"How much do you think it's worth? Gotta be a fortune!" Scottie grinned, stepping closer to the finger.

"I hope so." Daryl answered, glancing up at the setting sun. "…Getting kind of late now. Is your friend going to be at the museum tomorrow?"

"Yeah, should be. He's always working." Greg chuckled, "I know he'll find this fascinating. But if he can't exactly help you with the finger, I'm sure he can…*point* you in the direction of others who can! … Pun intended." He jabbed. Daryl nodded and grinned at the bad joke, while Scottie rolled his eyes.

"Hey, honey!" Jamie called, poking her head out from the front door. "Oh, hi guys!" She smiled, stepping out to greet the neighbors. After catching up with Greg and the kid, she turned to her husband.

"I'm sorry, honey, but can you run back to the grocery store? I started to pull everything out to cook dinner and realized I forgot to get garlic."

"Yeah, of course. I'll head out right now."

After saying his goodbyes to the neighbors, Daryl ran back down to the basement. As he gently placed it in the crate, he felt something hidden under the stuffing. It felt like paper. Pulling his hand out, he retrieved a small scroll that was buried inside. Faded ancient texts were written along the material. Daryl's eyes glistened in the dark room as he looked over the tattered scroll, wondering what it could possibly mean.

"You still down there, hon?" Jamie called. Daryl jumped, pulling him from his inquisitive trance. He placed the paper back inside the dusty crate and got to his feet. Flicking off the light, he climbed the stairs and made his way to the car.

"I'll be right back!" Daryl waved as he drove off down the road. As soon as he turned the corner out of sight, the skater ran back to the Frazer home and rang the doorbell. Jamie eventually opened the door to find the dancing boy on her welcome mat.

"Hey, Mrs. Frazer, could I use your restroom?" He frantically asked.

"Um, sure, Scottie." Jamie answered curiously, "Isn't your house just down the street, though?"

"Can't make it!" He cut her off.

"Okay, down the hall, to the right." She directed him. As the twelve-year-old waddled across the house, Jamie headed back towards the kitchen. Scottie stopped before the bathroom door and slowly turned back down the hall. Peaking around the corner, he watched as she lowered the heat on the stovetop and stirred the steaming pot.

Okay, gotta be quick. Where is that thing? Scottie wondered, searching the home.

Nearing the end of the hallway, a voice softly whispered in the boy's ear. He wanted to jump, but didn't. Something about it was so soothing that he barely budged. Looking around, his eyes rested on the basement door at the end of the hall. It was wide open with flickering lights illuminating the stairs. His feet felt weightless as they carried him down the hall. The whispers grew louder, bouncing around in his skull. Down below, the finger was waiting for him.

Gently picking the finger up, he felt the whispers fade away and the world came back into focus. Unsure of how long he had been wandering, he turned back and ran up the stairs. Sneaking down the hall and turning around the corner, he collided into Jamie.

"Woah, sorry, there you are!" Jamie jumped. "Everything okay?"

"Yeah, sorry…got lost wandering." Scottie answered nervously, stuffing the finger into his back pocket.

"Okay. Did you need anything else, Scottie…?" She began, but was cut off.

"No, no. I'm good. Thank you, Mrs. Frazer!" He smiled as he hastily made his way out the front door.

"Weird kid." Jamie shrugged.

"Hell yeah!" He whispered to himself with a grin. "Got it!"

Scottie ran over to his skateboard and jumped on. The wheels rattled down the driveway before he jumped off the lip and off into the street. With rich orange and blue clouds overhead, he watched as the sun was nearly set. Unable to wipe that smile off his face, he dreamed of everything he could have with the money that the finger would bring him. A new gaming setup, all the most valuable skateboards he could ask for, and chicks, of course. Debating what to tell his parents, he figured the best story he could come up with was that he found it in a crate on the side of the road.

Doesn't matter. Once they see how much it's worth…they won't mind a lil' old finders keepers!

Scottie's mind went blank. The last thing he felt was the sudden impact of cold steel on his left knee. The boy had cut across the alleyway without looking and did not expect a large truck to be driving his way. Without any time to stop, the truck ran the boy over. Coming to a skidding halt, the driver leapt out of his car—but it was too late. The middle-school skater was gone. His left arm had snapped backwards. Torn and bloody, it rested over his back pocket where he stashed the treasured mummy's finger.

———

Driving home in his ten-year-old blue Chevy, Daryl noticed that the "check engine" light flickered on once again. Ignoring it, he turned down his street, where he was greeted by several police cars. Daryl's heart sank, worried something happened to his wife. An officer waved his light, directing him where to drive. Passing by the police tape and the officer, he rolled down his passenger side window and leaned over.

"What happened, officer?" Daryl asked as his heart raced.

"Accident. Someone was run over..." He started.

"Oh God! I live down the road! My wife—is she okay?"

"Yes, sir. I'm sure she's alright." The officer sighed, "This was a child."

"Jesus! Scottie...!? How bad is he?"

"I'm sorry sir, but we need you to clear the road." The officer backed up, waving his hand. Daryl ignored the gesture.

"Did he make it to the hospital?"

"No, sir. He was killed on impact. There was nothing anyone could have done."

Daryl rolled back into his seat. He couldn't take his eyes off the blood that dripped from the grill of the truck, still sitting in the alleyway.

"Sir, I'm really sorry, but we need you to keep driving." The words came through his ears, muffled and distant. Daryl's throat went dry and his mind drifted off. Finally, he let go of the brakes and continued driving home. Pulling into the driveway, his wife opened the front door and stepped outside.

"Hey honey! Whoa, what's going on?"

"You didn't hear?"

"No, I was just getting everything ready until you came back with the…What happened?"

Daryl hugged his wife tightly. At a loss for words, he finally whispered, "Scottie was killed."

"What?! Scottie, down the road?" She pulled back, with eyes wide like the moon.

"Hit by a truck in the alleyway on his skateboard."

"Oh my God…" She spoke softly, overwhelmed, "What about his parents?! Do they know?"

"I'm sure the police…talked to them. I just told you what I know." Looking down into her eyes, he held his wife's hands tighter.

She pulled her husband closer, resting her head on his chest. "He was just over here…and now he's gone, just like that."

———

After loading the dishwasher, Daryl took the trash bag out of the bin and walked to the front door. Stepping down his driveway and onto the curb, he looked down the road at the alleyway where the accident occurred. The police cars were gone and so was the truck. Nothing left now, but the memory of the loss. Daryl tossed the bag into the trash bin and turned to head back inside.

"I'm going to bed, sweetie." Jamie said softly as she passed him by. She was unbuttoning her pants when she turned the corner into the bedroom. Daryl flicked off the living room light switch and stepped after her. Something stopped him. A funny feeling on the back of his neck. He looked back down the hall and spotted the basement door was wide open. The lights were off as the stairs descended into darkness.

"You coming, baby?"

Daryl's tense body jolted before letting out a breath and a chuckle. He answered, "Be right there, honey."

Turning his attention back to the basement, he reached for the light switch. The stairs were lit dimly, with one bulb dead and the other on the way as he descended into the basement.

I just changed those lightbulbs last week...

Reaching the bottom of the stairs, his eyes landed on the large crate ahead. It was still left open, but inside—something was different.

"What the he—"

The light shut off and Daryl was engulfed by the darkness. His heart raced as he backed up towards the stairs. Feeling out for a wall, he stumbled, landing harshly on the bottom steps. His back cracked as he struggled to his feet. Believing himself to be going mad, he heard whispers coming from the shadows. Voices in his head. Speaking a language he had not known. One he had never heard before. Unable to think or speak, all he could do was run. Daryl found his footing and sprinted up the stairs. The voices grew louder and closer behind him. It felt as though someone was leaning just over his shoulder. He could feel the chill in his ear. With a violent swing, he slammed the door shut behind him. The voices were gone. The house was silent.

"You okay?" Jamie called out.

His heart still racing, he took a breath and shook his head. "…Yeah, I'm fine, baby! Just… stumbled in the dark." He closed his eyes and took a deeper breath. He told himself he was just seeing things. It had been a hard day and his mind was over stimulated. Whatever was down there would be gone in the morning. He needed to sleep. Daryl looked down at the shut door behind him for another moment, before turning and heading to bed.

What laid in the large crate was not a finger. It was something more—a hand.

———

The next morning Daryl walked Jamie out to her car. With a kiss, she was off. Stepping back inside, Daryl slowly turned and walked down the hallway. The basement door was still shut ahead of him. He had to look. He had to prove it to himself that what he saw was all in his mind.

Cautiously outstretching his hand, he grasped the cool doorknob. Opening to the abyss, Daryl lingered in the doorway. Finally, he flicked the light switch to his side and the bulbs came to life—just as dim as the night before. He couldn't put it off any longer, he had to go. The boards creaked with every step he took. He waited for the whispers, but the basement remained silent.

Standing over the open crate, he looked down at the mummified hand. Overnight one finger had grown to a palm with a thumb and the remaining fingers—rotten and bandaged in cloth older than dirt.

This can't be real. It's not possible!

Daryl pulled the blue vinyl gloves tightly over his hands. The bland sanitary smell hovered under his nose as they snapped on his wrist. Wrapping the hand in the old cloth, he hustled back up to his car. Switching gears to reverse, he backed out onto the road and took off. Headed for the museum, he went over the story in his head. Eventually, he decided that he would leave out the part where the hand grew overnight. He didn't need these professionals thinking he was crazy. Eager to finally get some answers, he pressed down further on the gas pedal.

———

Arriving at the Natural History Museum, Daryl squeezed his car into a small spot on the street. After tossing a few quarters in the meter, he looked around and crossed the road, too impatient to run down to the crosswalk at the signal.

Whales. Ask for Mr. Whales. Or was it Doctor Whales?

Entering through the heavy front doors and crossing the large entry room, Daryl went straight for the front desk.

"Hi, I'm here to meet Dr. Whales…"

"Hello." Whales smiled as he walked over to the counter. The pudgy older man reached out and shook Daryl's hand. "Nice to meet you, Mr. Frazer. Come with me and we can take a look at your item."

With a gesture, Daryl followed the man down the hall and through two sets of doors. Turning a corner, they entered the research room with a large light-up table where they would inspect all of their artifacts. Daryl was surrounded by boxes and cabinets filled with files and other historical items and documents.

"Feels like area fifty-one back here." Daryl joked. "You guys got the Ark of the Covenant hidden in here?"

"No, sir." Whales chuckled as he slid on his gloves, "But we do have the fountain of youth stashed in the other room."

"Well, this may not be as special as that, but hopefully you can help me figure out what this thing is…" Daryl started as he slowly unwrapped the old, dusty hand. It seemed to smell worse each time he held it. For just being a hand, he almost got the feeling that it was watching him. Something wasn't right with this thing and he wanted to be rid of it.

"Wow. How did you say you found this?" Whales asked.

"It was in a crate…found it in the basement of the house we just moved into."

"Interesting." He whispered as he held the finger up closer to his face.

"Yeah, the owner had all kinds of strange things boxed up down there. Boxes of bugs, old scrolls and photos. Some kind of scientist or archaeologist maybe? I haven't quite figured him out yet. I just needed answers on this hand more than anything with all the weird things going on…"

"This appears to be part of one of the Tarim Basin mummies." Whales stated, almost in awe.

"How do you know that?"

"The inscription here on the scroll you brought in. It's not Egyptian." Whales turned his attention to Daryl, "…What weird things have been going on?"

"Oh, it doesn't matter. I think the hand has just been giving my wife and I the creeps."

"Okay, well, the skin looks to be paler. European. And from what I can read, the text appears to be the Tocharian language. Again, I'm no expert. I really could use other eyes on this—more experienced scholars, but what you have here may be a very rare and valuable discovery, Mr. Frazer."

Daryl's eyes lit up, imagining the growing dollar signs.

"It's regarded as a chapter of forgotten history. These mummies date back to 1800 B.C. Were they simply travelers moving across Asia? No one knows where they came from."

"What is that…?" Daryl asked, his smile fading.

"Looks like…blood under the fingernails." He paused before turning to look at Daryl with a concerned look in his eyes. "Fresh blood."

Daryl's phone loudly rang, startling the two men. He hastily reached into his pocket and pulled out the phone, reading his wife's name on the screen. Politely gesturing to the other man, Daryl answered the call.

"Hey, sweetie! How are…" He began, but was cut off by a sobbing voice on the other end of the phone. "What? Slow down. Please, honey, you're not making sense!"

Whales stood there unsure of what to do.

"Okay. Okay. I'll…I'll be right there!" He hung up the phone and buried it back in his pocket.

"I'm so sorry, I need to go. Some kind of emergency."

"No problem at all, Mr. Frazer. Are you going to be alright?"

"Yeah…thanks! I…here, ya know what? Keep the hand for now. Look it over and let me know if you find out anymore! I can come back by tomorrow, if you're around?"

"Yes. I'll be here. That sounds good to me. I'll take precious care of it! Drive safely, sir!"

After racing through traffic, Daryl pulled up to his driveway. Police cars were parked at their neighbor's home, while an ambulance had just pulled away. Its lights weren't flashing and the siren wasn't on.

Not a good sign.

Jogging up to the front door, Jamie opened it before he could reach the handle. With teary, red eyes, she hugged her husband.

"Oh God, it was so horrible!" She cried. "Greg…He fell off the roof. He was fixing the rain gutter when he tripped and landed on his head. I heard his neck…snap…from across the yard. It was the worst thing I've ever heard."

"I'm so sorry..." He whispered, in shock, holding his wife tighter.

"We were having an every-day conversation. I was out watering the grass, he was telling me all about his sister who's about to have a kid…" Jamie started sobbing. "He would have been…an uncle next month."

"I'm so sorry you had to see that, sweetie." Daryl rubbed her head as she wept against his chest.

"The worst part was…when he fell. After the snap…I could hear him muttering something. Almost whispering to me. His eyes were locked on me when I walked over to his body. I…I couldn't understand what he was saying, but it didn't sound like him. It sounded like an entirely different person. I haven't been able to stop shaking since, Daryl. I can barely breathe."

First Scottie. Now Greg. That hand…It had to be behind this.

The next morning Daryl was awoken by the ringing of his cell phone. Rubbing his eyes and outstretching his arm he retrieved it from the night stand.

"Hello?" The foggy-brained Daryl answered.

"Hello Mr. Frazer. ...Sorry, is this a bad time?"

He watched Jamie roll over to his right, but she remained asleep. "No. What's going on? Any news on the mummified fin—hand?"

"Yes. I had a peer who specializes in ancient mummifications investigate the remains. He was very fascinated by the hand, sir. We discussed the history of the region it originated from and the type of people this body part could be a remnant of..."

"What about the writing on the scroll?" Frazer interrupted.

"Well, the inscription is hard to read, but what we can make out so far is that it says something about those unworthy who touch this hand will trade their lives for the power of the worthy." Whales nervously stated. A moment passed as he waited for a response, but Daryl sat in silence on the other end.

"Are you still there, Mr. Frazer?"

"Yes. Yeah, I'm here." He hesitated. Daryl remembered Greg touching the hand when he was showing it off in the driveway. *Can it be real?* Tossing the thought aside, he rose from the bed and quietly walked out of the room.

I touched the hand too...but I was wearing gloves! Does that protect me?! This can't be real! I sound insane!

"You can keep the hand." He finally responded. "Consider it a donation."

"That's why I wanted to call you...We don't have it. I thought, perhaps, you came by earlier and collected it from another employee at the museum."

"You…don't have the hand?"

"No, sir." Whales answered. "…and it sounds like you didn't come to get it?"

"No."

"I'm so sorry, Mr. Frazer. I will have security check their footage and I will personally search every department in our museum for it in case it was displaced."

Frazer remained silent. Stunned. He stood at the bottom of the basement stairs looking down at the crate before him. Inside was not just a hand. Now it had grown a forearm.

"I will call you back with further updates. Again, I am sorry for the displacement. Hopefully, it is just stowed away somewhere here at the museum! Okay…have a good day."

Frazer hung up.

Pale, dry and crusty. The fingers had curled inward as if preparing to grasp something. It even looked more lively than before—As lively as a severed hand could look.

———

"Your story ain't making any sense, Mr. Frazer." Detective Borris shook his head.

"I told you everything. I swear to God, I am not making this up!" Daryl pleaded. The sockets around his red eyes were dark. Strands of hair hung over his pale face. He was barely holding it together after everything he had been through the last several weeks.

"So after two of your neighbors died, and this so-called mummy's finger grew into an entire arm—you and your wife fled?"

"Yes. We had to get away—for everyone's safety."

"…And you believe this mummy arm is responsible for the death of your wife, as well?"

"Yes." Daryl answered firmly. "I did not kill my wife!"

"Never said you did." The other detective spoke. "…But there is an awfully strange trail of bodies that you've left behind."

"And it's hard for us to believe a magic mummy hand is the culprit." Borris added.

"Not to mention that we can't find this thing anywhere." Detective Rains concluded. "You claim it was in your basement, but the place was empty."

"It's there…I know it's still down there." Daryl muttered as the sense of hopelessness washed over him. "Mummification was meant to preserve the body for all of time…but this body won't die! It wants to come back—and it won't stop unless we find it and destroy it!"

"You should be a horror writer saying things like that." The detective laughed.

———

A young boy ran through the empty structure, excited to explore his new home.

"This place is so cool!" The boy cheered.

The husband held his wife in the doorway as they watched their seven-year-old son sprint down the hall.

"I call this room!"

"Okay, Brendan." The mother giggled, "Just slow down. Don't want to hurt yourself!"

Brendan neared the end of the hall where the basement door creaked open. His curious eyes brought him closer to the dark stairway. Descending down the dimly lit steps, the boy discovered the crate sitting in the corner of the dark basement. As if in a trance, he stepped towards it. The boy was nervous, but he couldn't turn away. He had to see what was inside. The lid sat loosely over the crate, half open. The boy plugged his nose as the smell of rot radiated from inside. Using all of his muscles, he pushed the dense wooden lid off, revealing something in the dark. Not just an arm now, but the upper half of a mummified body. A decrepit, skeletal man. Pale and disfigured, its unhinged jaw rested open, as though it was about to scream. Dried blood ran down its face from the empty sockets dug into his skull. The Mummy's hand was outstretched towards the young boy—reaching for its next soul to take.

<u>COYOTES</u>

Slaughtered bodies baked under the blazing sun. Riley Russell laid bleeding in the dirt. The dry dessert air left his skin cracked as his ears were still ringing from the gunfire. Warm blood flowed down his arm from a gunshot wound in his left shoulder and another just above his hip. Loose bullets fell free from his vest as he rolled over onto his side. Shells littered the desert and the smell of gunpowder filled the air. With his nose nearly broken, he couldn't smell and could barely breathe. He tried to crawl away from the burning wreckage when he heard two men running his way. Firing a warning shot at the dirt beside him, the two men cautiously came out from behind one of the burning vehicles.

"Don't shoot! I have a message for El Sadico!" Russell shouted in Spanish.

The two men stood over him with their guns aimed at the back of his skull. One of them knelt down on Russell's back and retrieved zip ties from his pocket.

"We weren't going to kill you, gringo." The gunman growled, pulling the restrained man up to his feet. "But you're gonna wish we did when you see what the boss does to you, cabron!"

————

The sun was setting by the time the bullet-riddled Jeep made its way across the Mexican desert. Dark smoke billowed from the cranking engine as it struggled to complete its journey, passing through small towns and communities, before finally ending its trip in a small village known as *Arena Tranquila*—the home of El Sadico. It was nearly a ghost town before Sadico's takeover—what remained today was nothing more than a decrepit den of scum and villainy. Russell listened as the Jeep came to a stop before the doors flung open. A moment later he was yanked from his seat, stumbling to the ground.

"Get up!" The gangster shouted, grabbing him by the collar and dragging him along the dirt. Russell struggled to find his balance with his hands tied and his head under the dirty hood. Sweat ran down his temple, rolling into his eye. Even after months of hunting in these parts, his body still couldn't adjust to the heat. Rising to his feet, he was relieved that at least the pain in his shoulder was beginning to fade.

"Keep moving, puta!" The other cartel member spat, smacking Russell in the back of the head. Under the burlap sack, he could make out a large building ahead of him. Two more men carrying shotguns turned and removed the heavy metal barrier, swinging open the creaking doors.

"Welcome home." One of them laughed as the bleeding hostage passed by.

————

Russell was brought to his knees before the notorious kingpin. Tearing the burlap sack off of his head, his eyes slowly came to focus on the man standing over him. El Sadico smiled, revealing rotting teeth hiding under his dark mustache. His bald head gleamed under the faded-yellow bulbs. Gold and silver rings decorated his scarred and swollen fingers. The older man had ruled this dominion for many years, and in that time, several criminals had tried to take it from him—even some of his own allies from within. Those that were truly loyal to Sadico kept him alive. They knew what he would do to them if they were to betray their leader. El Sadico, which translates to *"The Sadist,"* was known along the border as one of the most brutal men the cartel had ever seen. Whispers of ghost stories spread among the locals of a man so evil, many thought of him as something supernatural.

The devil wouldn't have him. Some would say, which is why he lives to this day, controlling the trafficking into the United States. Politicians from California, New Mexico and other states would regularly meet with this man in the shadows. Billions of dollars passed back and forth through these walls each and every year, and the numbers were only growing. No members of the law in the states or Mexico would dare take him down. Sadico owned the border and there was nothing anyone could do about it.

The last police officers that even dared halt his trade were later found strung up in shipping containers with their eyes and tongues gouged out. Crime reports went on to list that their private parts were crammed down their throats and their bodies were littered with cuts and bruises. His torture methods would know no bounds and could last for days. El Sadico took pleasure in these acts. He loved watching the fear in their eyes grow when the realization hit that there was nothing they could do. They were his up until their final moments where he sent them off to Hell with the others.

One of Sadico's men grabbed Russell by the neck and pulled the dirty cloth loose that was tied around his mouth. The bitter taste of sweat and motor oil stained his dry tongue. Russell spat blood at Sadico's feet. The crimson dripped down his shining leather shoes. Sadico softly chuckled before swiftly kicking Russel in the teeth. The broken man's head rattled as he tasted blood dripping down his throat. The screaming nerves in his teeth ached along his jaw. Squeezing his eyes shut, he let the pain pass him over.

Soon it would all be worth it.

Sadico nodded his head and two of the gangsters swiftly stepped forward to tear off his bullet proof vest. One of them cut through the worn straps with his large hunting knife before cutting through the bleeding man's shirt and tearing it off. As the gangster took the items and tossed them aside, the other man noticed something strange. Blood had now dried on the hostage's sunburnt skin. The dried blood surrounded wounds that did not exist. The bullet holes in Russell's shoulder and hip were gone.

Was he seeing things? The gangster they called, Gilopollas thought to himself. Before he could speak, his leader waved him aside. Sadico had retrieved a rusty fire poker from a bin filled with weapons by his side. As he gripped the metal bar in his hands, all he could think about was whether he should use the baseball bat or crowbar afterwards. With a whole list of festivities planned for his new guest, Sadico was just getting started. He wanted all of his men around him to witness the repercussions one would receive for such bold actions.

The mobster slowly circled the hostage. His eyes looked him up and down like a hungry shark. Looming behind the kneeling man, Sadico sung back his arm before bringing it crashing down against Russell's back. Air and red spit fired from his lips. Russell couldn't breathe when his face crashed against the floor. For just a moment, he saw Susie lying there on the floor smiling back at him. Sadico's shining shoes stepped into view and the woman was gone. In a flash the leather shoe came rushing at his face. Russell's head rang back in a burst of agony. His body rolled like a rag doll onto his back. Beyond the ringing in his skull, he could hear the laughter of the men surrounding him.

Was this what she felt? What her final moments were like?

"I'm not here for the drugs. I'm not here for the guns." Russell began. The gang members around him chuckled. Sadico silenced them, not taking his eyes off of the hostage.

"I'm here for the women and the children." Rising back up to his knees, he spat dark blood on the floor. "Not just the ones you have now, but the ones that you've killed. Countless innocent lives…wasted. One of which—was my friend…My wife. Susie. Susie Russell. You, Sadico…You took her from me!"

A subtle grin grew along Sadico's lips. He had no idea who this man or his wife were. He didn't care. This was far from the first vengeful widow he had encountered, however, this man was the biggest nuisance of them all.

"She went out for a walk. Jogging like she would always do. I should have gone with her…I was tired. I…" Tears formed in the raging man's eyes. "They found her body…pale and bloody, left floating in the river along the border. When I held her for the last time…she was so cold. Now I can barely remember the last time we embraced—truly embraced. Her warmth…gone. Because of you—all I can feel now is that lifeless, bitter, cold."

Russell's hateful eyes never left Sadico. He watched the cocky smile grow on the old man's face. He enjoyed his story, but he wasn't going to like how it ended.

"Now I'm going to take everything away from you. Every single thing. Until finally, I will take your life. You miserable, scum-sucking, heartless mother-fu —"

A cartel member beat him over the back of the head with his shotgun. Russell simply laughed through the pain. His vision blurred, but began to change. He started to see colors in different ways. The men surrounding him began to glow as he could feel the heat radiating off of them.

"It's funny…all my time in the desert. Tracking your people… I learned a lot. I finally nailed my Spanish and now I know the sun and the sand like the back of my hand. I also learned enough to really make an impact in your operations. I was really close to tracking you down too… but then I was attacked one night. Not by your men, but by an animal. A wolf. Biggest thing I've ever seen. I killed it—barely survived myself…"

Russell writhed in pain, falling to his hands and knees. His neck cracked as his head rolled back. Blood dripped from the sinister smile that stretched along his laughing face. Bones slowly began to twist and crack under his skin. Some of the men noticed and slowly started to back away.

"Before that night—I had a chance at killing you. But now… after what I've become… there's not a chance in Hell that you survive to see the sunrise!"

Sadico's eyes grew wide, watching in horror as the stranger began his metamorphosis. The muscles along his limbs rippled and grew as his arms and legs extended beyond belief. His boney fingers snapped as they bent and contorted. The skin under his fingernails bled as they grew longer and sharper. Sadico watched the laughing man's face. The color of his eyes faded from a rich green to a golden yellow—almost glowing in the dark den. His heart raced, but his body wouldn't budge. He couldn't believe what was happening in front of him. Many of his men stood in shock as others took off running. Some of them cocked their guns and got ready to fire.

Bullets were unloaded into the stretching, peeling flesh of the gringo. Piercing the skin, they drew blood—but the man barely flinched. His skin grew darker as hair erupted from his pores, and with that came loose the fresh bullets. They bounced along the concrete floor like hail in a thunderstorm. The laughing that boomed from his throat deepened and altered, sounding nothing like the man he once was. Now he was becoming an animal—a werewolf!

The wolf rose to his feet, standing over a foot taller than anyone else inside. Thick drool dripped from dagger-like teeth that peered through its vile grimace. The beast snapped to its right, gripping a gunman's wrist with its claws. In an instant the man's hand was torn off and blood spewed in the air. The man's screams were quickly silenced when the wolf lunged forward, biting down into the flesh of his neck. With a snap, the gangster's body fell limp. The wolf tossed him to the side. Before his body hit the wall with a loud thud, the wolf turned back and grabbed another shooter by the throat. Lifting him up in the air, he desperately fired his pistol into the wolfman's ribs. It roared, biting into his face. Screams turned to gurgles before the wolf peeled the flesh away from his spasming skull.

With blood dripping down its face, the wolf licked its putrid lips. A dozen more bullets were expunged from the bleeding flesh of the wolf. Already healing, it stepped over the bodies. The beast's gnarly, long snout sneered as it sniffed the drug den. Most men had given up shooting, and ran for the exits. Sadico was gone, but the wolf would find him. Russell wasn't letting anyone live to see the sunlight.

Sadico screamed for his men, shoving them down the hallway as he passed. His heart beat out of his chest as his lungs struggled to take in air. For the first time in years—the kingpin was frightened. For once, he wasn't at the top of the food chain. Desperate for every meat shield he could find, he pushed his way deeper into the underground caverns of his base of operations. He could hear the wolf's blood-curdling howl, ringing out through the halls. The night was young and the hunt had only just begun.

Sniffing the air, Russell sensed another man in the next room over. That's when he heard the click of a revolver being loaded. In a flash, the wolf crashed through a brittle wooden wall, where he took hold of the fat cartel member hiding in the corner named, La Mierda. The stench of the gangster's sweat stung Russell's nostrils. Faded tattoos ran down his face, surrounding the eyeballs that bulged out of his head. The beast's claws pierced through his chest, tearing away at his vile, beating heart. Another gangster kicked open the door, wielding two pistols. Before he could take the shot, the wolf tossed the slimy heart across the room, hitting the man in the face. He flung himself back, choking on blood that hit the back of his throat as he flailed the guns in his hands. Nearly firing at himself in a panic, it was over before he could get his footing. The werewolf crossed the room, gripping the man by the throat. The gangster muttered something in Spanish, before the wolf crushed his frail neck like a juice box.

Finally reaching the back of the large building, Sadico spotted the doorway to some of the emergency tunnels his men had dug for him years ago. He owned the police, but he always had to keep an eye out for other criminals. Any up and coming kids would be eager to take his throne. If he couldn't kill them all, he would certainly escape them. The frantic kingpin slammed the metal door behind him, descending into the dimly lit tunnels. Several men with machine guns and machetes came rushing down the halls, searching for the attacker. Many of them were unaware of what they were truly going up against. Some of his cartel soldiers stayed back, barricading the steel door with crates and tables, nailing wooden beams across the frame—Anything they could do to slow down the creature.

Charging down the dusty hall, Russell could see the barricaded door ahead. He heard the sounds of several panicked men shouting at each other as they frantically loaded their guns. Their thunderous beating hearts rang out like dinner bells for the werewolf. The promising taste of boiling raw flesh was irresistible. The wolf would have his bloodshed. These men were just the appetizers.

Russell's claws tore away at the barricaded wall. Sharp fangs gnawed down on the wood as he flung pieces across the room. Nothing was stopping him from getting to Sadico. The men began firing. Cutting through his fingers like a million paper cuts, the wolf pulled back. Before he could kick down the door, three smugglers came rushing down the hall from behind him. Swinging his machete, he brought it down into the wolf's bicep. With a howl, he clenched his fists. The wolf's golden eyes locked onto the attacker, and with a violent swing of his bleeding arm, he sent the criminal flying back against the stone wall. A scream and a loud crack, before the man's body fell silently and limply on the floor.

One of the other men, dark-skinned with a short mohawk, turned and ran. The wolf could taste the tears forming in his eyes as he disappeared down a dark hallway. The other, a middle-aged man with a graying beard and tear drop tattoos, fired his desert eagle at the wolf's gut. The impact sent the wolf back a few steps, nearly toppling over. It burned, but Russell wasn't stopping. Before he could unload his gun on the beast, the bearded man was nothing but a puddle of blood and muscle on the floor.

The wolf took a breath. Gazing at the carnage that surrounded him. Six months ago, Russell was working as armed security in El Paso, and now he was standing in a pile of steaming intestines. His blood-soaked wounds burned, his broken bones ached, but Russell kept telling himself it was only temporary. As his monstrous body slowly healed, he lumbered forward, fighting the urge to eat the warm remains at his feet.

Hector, a man with a long pony tail and two missing fingers—one from playing with fireworks, and the other for cheating on his wife—came rushing into the room with a grenade launcher. The cartridge was launched down the hall, crashing into the wolf's chest. A ball of fire erupted, shattering glass and sending the beast flying through the air. He was launched across the room, crashing through the wall, and back against a large shelving unit filled with boxes. A sudden burst of white smoke filled the room. His nose twitched as he fought for air—inhaling much of the substance. Millions of dollars worth of cocaine had erupted from the boxes and descended on the beast like a blizzard in the humid cave.

The powdery white werewolf's pupil's dilated and its muscles tingled as the drugs ran through his system. The beating of his heart continued racing, as the hair on his body stood tall. He truly felt unstoppable now, letting out a guttural howl that shook the foundation of the crumbling lair. Some men around him, covered in the white powder, took off and ran. The others reloaded their guns and fired. Russell charged, yanking the rifle free of his hand and shoving it back into his face. The criminal's jaw was shattered in one brutal swing.

Behind the wolf, came another attacker, swinging a blood-stained hatchet down into the shoulder of the beast. Russell shrieked and swung his arm back, reaching for the man. He pulled the hatchet back out, dodging the claws rushing towards his head. Staying hidden behind the shuffling beast, he brought it down a second time into its shoulder blade. Russell hissed, swinging around and finally making contact. He gripped the man's left thigh. Pressing tightly, his claws dug deeper into his skin. Blood pooled in the man's pant leg as he screamed, cursing at the sky. Russell's heart thudded like a locomotive as he tore the man's leg loose from his body. Skin and tendons ripped as blood gushed. Soon the man's screams turned to silence as he passed out on the floor.

One more killer came sprinting out from the dark. He had a bat with nails at the end of it over his head, ready for the kill, but the wolf was faster. He swung the dismembered leg, clashing into the man's head. A wet crunch was heard before the limp body crashed down onto the dusty floor. The man's head was crushed like a soda can, pooling in his own filth on the ground.

Intoxicated by the rush, the wolf's eyes rapidly darted, his body swung and twitched as he searched his surroundings. Sensing a break in the action, he went back for the barricaded door. Instead of pulling back at the barriers, the beast simply charged it. Through an eruption of dust and debris that rattled the home, the wolfman broke past the barrier and continued rushing down the dark hallway. Sadico would soon be his.

––––––––

The cold glow of a full moon pierced through the dark clouds overhead. Sadico stumbled, climbing out of a nearby cellar door. Free of the dark tunnels, he sprung to hit feet and searched for a car—but they were gone. The few men smart enough to leave, ran off and took the cars. Tire tracks ran off into the darkness of the desert, leaving their helpless leader behind.

"Cowards!" He shouted, cursing his men.

The desperate crime lord's eyes darted, searching for somewhere to hide. Sadico's mind wandered, imagining all the things he would do to those men. Bodies would hang from trees if he survived this night. Nothing would stop him from tracking the gutless pigs down. Rage fueled him stronger than any drug could. The cigar-smoking man's lungs wheezed as he ran through the quiet village streets. He could have asked for help if he hadn't killed and enslaved what was left of the citizens.

The wolf burst through the hatch and out onto the surface. He basked under the moonlight as the dust settled around him. Sniffing at the night air, he caught a whiff of his prey. The wolf's ears perked up as he heard the killer calling out for help. Sadico was running from building-to-building, banging on locked doors, begging his people for sanctuary. No one answered his calls. The beast let out a bone-chilling howl that roared throughout the village. The muscles in Sadico's back tightened as chills ran down his spine. He was running out of options.

Russell ran through the small village, hot on the trail of his next meal. Sadico was close. He could hear his heart racing. Soon the killer's dark blood would be dripping from his lips. The wolf turned the corner into a clearing from the ghost town. Up ahead on the hill was a lone chapel, crumbling into the desert. A sinner's only hope at the end of the line. The only doors that would welcome a man like him, when they deserved to be locked.

"You dare beg for God's mercy?!" The wolf growled, kicking open the doors with a bang that rattled the fragile foundation.

Cobwebs filled the rafters of the quiet church. Thick layers of dust lingered along the rows. Scattered along the stone floor were the melted remains of old candles. Beams of moonlight cut through the shattered stained-glass windows above, bringing light to the empty, black building. Kneeling before the altar, at the other end of the building, was Sadico. He was hunched over, weeping. The wolf felt nothing for him.

"Heaven won't take you, but I'll make sure Hell does!" The beast spat with his thunderous voice.

Sadico flipped around, wielding a processional cross. In a flash, he lunged forward, impaling the wolf's chest with the metal cross. The beast cried, stumbling backwards.

"Die, diablo!" He screamed, pressing the beam further into the creature's flesh. A wicked smile stretched across his bloody face. "Rot in Hell!"

Russell roared through the pain, kicking back at his attacker. His clawed foot quickly kicked at Sadico's gut, knocking the wind out him and sending his body across the chapel. Brittle wooden pews shattered as he passed through them. Dust filled the air while the man choked on the floor, rolling in pain. The wolf slowly rose to his feet, groaning through his clenched teeth. Quickly, he pulled the cross back out of his chest with a miserable roar, and flung it across the room. The weeping Sadico flinched on the dirty floor when the metal cross rang out like a gunshot as it hit the stone walls. Russell grinned thinking of all the bones that Sadico had broken.

They wouldn't be the last.

Picking the criminal up by the collar, he tore through the expensive fabric of his new suit. Before Sadico could beg through bleeding lips, the wolf spun, launching him across the room once again. Sadico screamed with a crack in his spine as his broken body crashed against the altar of the church. Struggling to get up, he desperately limped along the floor. His nerves trembled to his core as he heard the sound of the wolf stomping towards him.

"This isn't over!" Sadico cursed as he clumsily got to his feet. He knew that if he was dying tonight, he wasn't going out without a fight.

The wolfman swiftly swung his claws at the mobster, cutting through his jacket. Sadico pounced behind the alter, landing in agony—but briefly out of reach. Russell raised the podium over his head, before bringing it crashing down onto the leader's legs. A thunderous snap echoed along the rotting stone walls. Letting out a blood-curdling scream, Sadico cursed in Spanish and spat at the beast. The older man rocked on the floor, bloody fingers grabbing at his shattered legs.

Can't run away anymore.

Russell leaned down and firmly grabbed his shattered ankle. Sadico wailed as he was slowly dragged down the aisle and back out through the chapel doors. The moon loomed over them like a spotlight, shining down on the monster being brought to justice. Mumbling as blood dripped down his face, Sadico begged for mercy.

"I'll give you anything you want. Money, drugs, women! As much as you could ever want— Ever dream of!" He pleaded.

The wolf ignored him.

"You can have it all! My enterprise! Take it! Just let me live! I'll run and you'll never see me again!"

Russell gripped Sadico's trembling throat with his clawed hand. He lifted the gangster up, slamming his body against a large metal shipping container. Snot ran down the nearly-crying criminal's face. The wolf's ears shifted, ignoring the begging brutalist, when he heard something shuffling inside that container. With his other hand, he swung his dagger-like claws downward, slicing through the chains that locked the doors.

When the metal latch swung open, Russell was greeted with a retched odor leaking from the large box. He leaned his head inside, spotting eyes staring back at him. Shivering figures in the dark. Children. Dozens of them. Thin to the bone. Starving and chained to the floor. A bloody mattress laid at the center of the container with filth-filled buckets to the side. The frightened children clustered together back against the wall, hiding in the shadows, away from the large wolfman. Russell's grip tightened around the throat of the monster. Sadico's slimy skin was turning blue when he looked back over at him. He could have killed him at that moment—but that was too easy.

————

Russell cautiously helped the nervous children out of the container. He explored the facilities, searching for any other innocent people locked away. Finally locating a kitchen in the base, he fed the children. Once he made sure they all were given food and water he left them, reminding them to stay put. Ensuring them that they were safe. Small smiles spread along their sunken-in cheeks. The boys and girls head each other close. They had been through worse than anything Russell could imagine. That's when he made his way back to Sadico.

The werewolf grabbed the broken body of the crime lord that he had left hanging upside down from a forklift. The brittle bones in his legs cracked as Russell shifted his body. Sadico cried out, swinging his restrained arms at the beast. Ignoring the weak man's feeble attacks, he swung the body across the dirt and into the dirty shipping container. Sadico landed with a thud that boomed inside the empty box. Groaning through broken teeth, he rolled on the floor, not noticing the dark puddles around him. Russell retrieved a gangster's golden lighter and flicked it on. The flame danced in his beastly hand. As he tossed it in the air, Sadico noticed a familiar smell in the air. Gasoline.

Plastic gas containers were sprawled along the dark corners of his metal tomb. With a gasp, he struggled to his feet, but his legs gave out, sending him back down to the ground. The old man slammed his jaw against the wet metal. Through blurry vision, he watched as the beast slammed the container door shut behind him, leaving Sadico in utter darkness. His only light—the flickering flame—quickly descended before him. In an instant, the box erupted in a blaze.

The flickering flames roasted the flesh of the monster inside. Staggering as he stepped away from the burning crypt, the wolf's bones ached and creaked. Clumps of hair fell to the ground as golden eyes faded back to green. Russell collapsed to his knees as he thought of his wife. Through all the screams, the blood, and dismemberment, he could still remember her laugh. The warmth of a new day wasn't the same as holding her in his arms, but it was a start. The wolfman watched the sun rise as Sadico's final agonizing screams rang out across the desert.

<u>COFFIN</u>

Eyes fluttered open in a pitch-black world. A young woman, sweaty and aching, shifted in the dark. It was tight with not much room for movement. She felt walls around her, and braces on her limbs. She stretched and pulled, unable to shift out of the position she was in. She was naked, laid out on her back. Blood pumped rapidly through her veins. The world was silent except for the sounds of her heart beat booming like thunder in her skull. She rolled her arms, feeling something pulling at her skin. As her eyes adjusted she could see the medical equipment running up and down her body attached to her limbs and torso. Needles and tubes were protruding from her flesh.

"Oh God, someone help me!" She pleaded. Her throat was sore and dry. "Anyone!? Help me, please!"

She tried fighting her restraints, shifting inside the dark chamber as much as she could. The metal was as cold as ice against her skin. Her teeth chattered while goosebumps spread across her body. Everything hurt. Then she noticed something else. With what little movement her head could make, she looked down at her feet. But she couldn't see them. Instead she discovered her stomach. It was large, extending far out from the rest of her body. Her insides churned as she came to a horrifying realization.

I'm pregnant!? I can't be! That's…impossible!

The woman screamed. She kicked and spat, but there was nothing she could do. She couldn't even reach her arms inward to touch her baby. Then, in the dark, she witnessed a shift under her flesh. The baby was moving inside her. She could almost make out the shape of the foot as it kicked against her gut. Both beautiful and horrifying, the young woman was overcome by her nerves. She could barely think straight with so much going on all at once.

"What the Hell is going on here!?" The mother panicked. "Let me out! Please!"

Nothing. The world stayed silent.

"I need help! Someone please! My name is…"

She couldn't remember. Her eyes danced in her sockets as she searched her mind for answers. She had none. She couldn't remember who she was.

How did I end up here? I must have gotten hit on the head…or something. She tried to come up with anything. Reasoning how she got pregnant. What she was doing earlier that day. She didn't even know what day it was. *Dammit I have to remember something!* She scolded herself.

A surge of pain shot through the young woman's body. She clenched her jaw, screaming through teeth. The restraints locked her trembling legs in place as she felt her water break.

The baby can't be coming already?! ...I don't even know what to do!

The young woman panicked, breathing rapidly as her insides burned and cramped. With no other choice, she started to push. She used every muscle in her body to push. Taking deeper breaths, she tried to focus. Her skin was burning up and her head was aching. All she wanted to do was tear those tubes out of her arms and legs. She wanted out of this cage— out of this nightmare. Sweat ran down her face as her long messy hair clung to her neck. Her heart raced as the walls seemed to close in on her.

This is no place to have a baby.

She kept pushing. As the pain grew worse, she closed her eyes. Flashes shot through her mind. Images of her family. Her life. She saw her mother. Her father. Her friends from school and teachers over the years. It was coming back. She saw glimpses of her graduation. She could smell the flowers in the family garden. She could taste the first beer she shared with her dad. The only sense of warmth inside this dark chamber flooded her mind and danced through her body.

I wish they were here with me...

Then it finally came back. She remembered a name. Her name.

Veronica!

A guttural scream of agony rattled through her throat as she gave one final push. Her lungs burned as the oxygen was all let out. She couldn't breathe. She couldn't stop pushing until the baby was out. Her limbs trembled as her nails dug into the flesh of her palms. It hurt even more than she ever imagined.

The baby's cries finally rang out. The sounds rattled off the walls of the small container they were crammed inside of. The woman took in a deep breath and sighed with a laugh.

I did it!

With her body still restrained, Veronica couldn't reach her baby. She couldn't hold it. She couldn't even tell if it was a boy or girl.

"I want to hold my baby, you monsters! Let me out! Please, I'm begging you!"

She felt the warm wetness of the infant rolling between her legs as it continued screaming.

"We need to hurry or my baby will die!" She pleaded with tears running down her face. "Now, God damn you!"

Another shot of pain ran up her leg.

"Ahhh!" She cried, looking down past her belly. "My baby…are you okay…Ow—Ouch! Jesus!"

The pain increased in her right thigh. It stung like a hornet, but it felt worse—like multiple stingers.

Teeth?! Is my baby biting me?

With a crunch the baby bit deeper into her meaty thigh. She screamed, now panicking. The baby bit deeper before flinging its head back, tearing the flesh away from her leg. She could feel her warm blood spewing everywhere. Bolts of pain shot across her nerves like lightning bolts in a storm.

"Oh my God!" Veronica cried. "Help me! God, help me! Someone—!"

Veronica felt the baby's tiny fingers sliding up to her hips. A moment later, she looked down to finally she her baby's face. It was staring back at her from under her belly. The baby's skin was ghostly pale and its eyes were dark. Lifeless. It was unlike any baby she had ever seen before. Before she could speak, the baby leaned its head back and opened its jaw. Teeth. Razor sharp teeth protruded from the infant's red gums. The baby bit down into her inflated stomach. Veronica moaned in agony, unable to do anything under attack. More blood oozed from the teeth marks, dripping down her naked, sweat-soaked body.

The mother bit at her cheek, fighting through the pain. Blood dripped down her fists as she dug deeper into her palms. The baby pressed its slimy head against her stomach, biting deeper into her. Blood gushed down the baby's throat, drenching its small body in the dark. Veronica laid there crying. She looked down at her baby wishing this was all a dream.

I remember wanting a baby one day when I was a little girl. I remember thinking of names. I remember wanting a little boy. She thought, doing her best to ignore the pain. *I finally got my baby…But I don't know what you are.*

Veronica titled her wrist, outstretching her fingers towards her child as it feasted on her guts. For a moment her finger grazed the backside of her baby.

It's warm and so soft. It felt like I always dreamed it would.

Veronica couldn't hold back the pain anymore. She felt her limbs beginning to go numb. Her energy was fading. Her eyelids grew heavy as the blood loss worsened. She ran her finger tip along the back of her monstrous infant as it began clawing at her flesh with its small fingers. It tore her wide open, biting at her intestines and consuming her insides. The baby was hungry and it wasn't stopping.

My baby…What have they done to you?

Veronica's final screams could be heard from outside of the shaking container. It was a compact black metal box. The same size as a coffin. It hung from a metallic conveyor belt along with several other coffins. The mother's agonizing screams joined the chorus of many others. Inside this dark factory from hell, stood figures dressed in black. Rubbery hazmat suits with dark gas masks and goggles lingered before the trembling coffins. One of them hastily jotted something down onto his clipboard. Another figure leaned forward, pressing a button and speaking into a microphone.

"Bring in the next round of patients."

<u>OVER AND BENEATH US</u>

"Those damn hippies are back again already?" Jenkins grumbled. "I swear that circus comes to town sooner each year…"

Sheriff Douglas Jenkins scowled as he passed by several people setting up tents and tables for the annual UFO festival. It was a plague brought upon his little town of Walton, Nevada every year as far as he was concerned. Jenkins was a no-nonsense kind of man. Nearing sixty-years-old, he had a short fuse with an explosive temper. Folks in these parts knew not to mess with the sheriff.

He turned the wheel and rounded the corner out, tossing his burning cigarette out the window. Jenkins watched the sun as it descended lower along the horizon, knowing his shift was over when it was down. The heat had been unbearable that week and the A/C on his patrol car was acting up. Not to mention, his wife grew more bitter every night he came home. The sheriff didn't mind his job, but he was in no mood to deal with the crazies this week. Last year they arrested a couple for indecent exposure in the desert, claiming they were attempting to be abducted. Year before that, an old man was spitting gibberish to locals in town, going on and on about lights in the sky and voices in his head. He resisted arrest, hitting one of the officers, and found himself in the town's jail for quite some time.

Jenkins clenched his wheel tighter as he drove. The speedometer rose—as did his blood pressure—pressing further down on the gas pedal, eager to return to bed after a longer than usual day. Quitting smoking was worse than he imagined. He narrowed it down from a pack a day to just three cigarettes. One after each of his meals—but that wasn't enough. Jenkins wasn't sure how much longer he could do it for.

"All officers, we have a 10-66. Suspicious individual in the area. Reports of a naked woman wandering the west side neighborhoods. She was last spotted on Cherokee Drive, headed south—out of town."

"Copy that, dispatch. I'm on my way." Jenkins answered. "Here come the crazies." He muttered to himself as he took off down the road.

———

Jenkins spent the next twenty minutes driving down Cherokee Drive and several other neighboring streets. No sign of the woman. Up ahead, he caught an older lady walking her small dog along the sidewalk. Jenkins pulled over besides the older woman and leaned his head out the window.

"Hello, ma'am. Have you spotted any strange individuals wandering the area?"

"No…nothing odd here, officer." She answered with a wavering voice. "Is the stranger dangerous?"

"Unsure of that ma'am, but it's safest for you to stay indoors for now. Call the police if you spot anything unusual."

"Thank you, sir." She waved.

"Have a goodnight, miss." He nodded and drove off. As he headed further south, leaving the neighborhood behind, Jenkins shook his head, realizing where she was going.

Another stupid hippie headed to Area 51…

―――――

Driving along the dusty outskirts of Walton, where the paved roads turn to dirt, Jenkins watched as the sun vanished beyond the horizon. Out in the Nevada desert, away from humanity, the stars brightly twinkled against the darkness of space overhead. A smile creaked along the corner of Jenkins' lip, reminiscing on nights of the past, laying in the bed of his truck with his date, watching for shooting stars in the night skies. So many years ago, yet the stars never changed, but the world below never seemed to stop.

Jenkins never thought that he'd end up as the grouchy old man in town, but here he was. Walton was his home, and he intended to keep it that way. He was born on this soil, and he damn well was getting buried in it.

"Holy Hell…" He choked, spotting a figure walking down the dirt road. It was the naked woman. He drove up closer behind her, with his glowing headlights highlighting the pale woman in the dark. Unaware, or intentionally ignoring him, she continued slowly walking ahead. Her slender, naked body glimmered in the dark. Her skin was coated with something that dripped from her fingertips with every step. Something strange. It was dark and thick like a slime or sludge, but it didn't look like oil or tar. Jenkins wasn't sure what it could be.

"Hello, ma'am! This is the Walton Police!" He called out.

No response. She kept on walking forward.

"Ma'am. This is the police!" He repeated, growing impatient. "Please, stop walking!"

Her thin legs wobbled, nearly buckling, as she stepped along the dirt. A shining trail of slime followed her down the dark road. He noted that the suspect appeared to be in her late-twenties with no signs of tattoos or birthmarks—and besides the strange substance coating her body—she looked to be unharmed.

"Alright, enough of this." He muttered as he pushed the brakes and shifted into park. The officer stepped out of the vehicle and slowly approached the woman, with his hand at his side, resting on his holster.

"Miss, stop right now or I will use force." He commanded.

Never flinching, she ignored his warnings and continued. He noticed that her arms and fingers twitched strangely while her dark mangled hair danced on her shoulders as strands clung to her wet, sappy flesh.

"I've had enough of these damn hippies tripping on acid in my town." He growled as he retrieved his nightstick from his belt. "Final warning, lady!"

Raising the baton, he stepped closer, ready to hit the back of her knees. Before he could make contact, the woman turned around and screamed. She was rigid like a machine, with a cry that rang out louder than any woman he had ever heard before. Jenkins stumbled back, partially covering his ears. A moment later, she dropped to her knees, sobbing uncontrollably. She cried out in another language. Speaking so rapidly, Jenkins couldn't understand a word she was saying.

Spanish? She a border jumper? He thought to himself. As she continued to cry in the dirt, feeling as though she wasn't a threat, he stepped towards her.

"It's alright, ma'am." He put his arm out, waving her towards him. "I can get you help. Come with me and we'll get this settled."

Strands of thick drool and snot ran from her whimpering face. Her forehead scrunched as her lip quivered, still rambling in an unknown language. Jenkins aimed his flashlight at her face, revealing her bloodshot eyes. Her eyes were a pale blue, wide and lost, as though she was glaring far beyond the cop and his vehicle, at some unknown horrors hidden in the endless darkness ahead.

He took another step forward, but she fell back —cowering in fear. Her limbs trembled as sludge dripped down her skin. Jenkins looked over at his patrol car and then back to the horrified stranger.

"Alright. One second, let me grab you something, Miss." He shuffled back to the trunk of the car and opened it, retrieving a blanket. Cautiously stepping closer to her, he opened the blanket wide to comfort her. Still muttering in her foreign tongue, she accepted the officer's arms as they wrapped the blanket around her. Then he noticed something strange on the left side of her skull—a small part of her head was shaved around some kind of surgical scar hidden behind her left ear. Jenkins' hand grazed her wet shoulder as he helped her to her feet. Goosebumps crawled across the woman's chilling flesh and his own.

Jesus! She's as cold as ice. He gasped, rubbing his still cold fingers together as he walked her back to the patrol car. *She must be part of the human trafficking at the border.* Jenkins sighed. *She managed to escape and now this girl's lost and scared out of her damn mind... Poor thing.*

"Right this way, ma'am. In the back. There ya go."

She shivered as she gripped the blanket, pulling it tighter around her slim figure. Her breathing had slowed and her cries had dampened to whispers. Her messy hair ran over her tired eyes, clinging to her clammy cheekbones. Gently rocking back and forth, she mumbled to herself as Jenkins closed the door behind her. As he climbed back into the driver's seat, he softly comforted her, "Let's get you back to the station. Everything is going to be alright."

Reaching forward and retrieving his radio, he brought it to his lips, but before he could say anything —a strange sound rattled from the speaker. It started as a low hum. A frequency that quickly heightened to an ear-piercing electronic scream. Jenkins dropped the radio and covered his ears. The woman jolted to life in the back, kicking at the front seat and screaming. The sounds from her tongue rapidly changed from one language to another. Jenkins recognized German and Russian, and others—but nothing in English.

"Hey! Stop that! Stop that right now and relax!" He ordered. Jenkins reached for his radio once again and spoke into it. "Dispatch, this is Jenkins, I found that naked woman…"

Something was wrong. The radio wasn't on. Jenkins flipped the power switch on and off, checking the channels and the other controls, but it wasn't working. The radio was dead.

"What in the holy hell is going on here tonight?!" He whispered, trying not to panic.

A loud crash banged behind the older man's head. It was the metal barrier between him and the back seat. The woman had slammed her head against it. Pulling her body back, she jerked forward and slammed her face into the cage again. Then again, and again. Blood oozed from the dangling sliced flesh of her forehead, dripping down her crying face that shuddered in the dimly lit car.

"Stop that!" Jenkins begged. " You're hurting yourself!"

She screamed in foreign tongues as she bashed her face in harder and faster. The cold metal tore at the stranger's flesh like a cheese grater, peeling away layers of her once soft features. The car shook with her relentless force. Until finally, she stopped. Blood spurted from her shredded cheekbone onto the cop's sleeve. Sitting there, frozen in terror, he watched the woman choke on her tears and blood. The next words that left her lips were finally in English, where she simply said:

"*They* took me."

She blinked, before collapsing in the back seat. With that, the vehicle shut off. The engine was killed and the lights went out. Jenkins tried turning the key, keeping his eyes locked on the woman in the rear-view mirror. The blanket fell from her slimy body as she began convulsing and twitching on the back seat.

"Jesus Christ!" He finally spat, struggling to open the door and rise to his feet.

The headlights blinked on and off as the police car shook back and forth. The red and blue lights flashed on the roof while the siren burst to life with its cries echoing across the empty dunes. The woman flailed and swung her body back and forth inside the patrol car. Jenkins reached for the door handle before she slammed her head against the window, cracking the glass. He jolted back away from the car, in shock of what he was witnessing.

"Lights from above...and below." She whispered as blood ran down her broken face. "Over...and beneath us."

The woman slammed her body against the glass in an inhuman way, breaking her nose and two of her fingers with a harsh snap. Bending backwards against the shattered window, her fingers twitched as if waving at the horrified old man. Thick black slime dripped from her lips as she choked out four final words.

"They'll…take…you…too."

The woman's pale blue eyes rolled up inside her skull as her lips danced with incredible speed—speaking words that didn't sound human. The police car's lights flashed and the siren wailed on and off as the girl inside bent and contorted until her pale flesh began to tear. Jenkins' stomach churned as her body changed form, folding in on itself and breaking. Something new was birthed from the torn flesh of her arms.

New appendages burst out from the bloody stumps—long and spindly like those of an insect. Stretching several feet—these spider-like legs kicked at the windows of the car. Her jaw had descended, unhinged from her skull, as she was screaming out into the night. The windows erupted, sending shards of glass through the air. With red-ish flesh like lobsters, the black slime oozed from the cuts and slashes, and her gaping mouth. Strands of thin dark hair descended from the balding woman's shriveling scalp as her several limbs twitched and her eyes bulged from within her crunching transforming skull.

It was a symphony of agony and Jenkins had front row tickets.

With white knuckles, he raised his gun and fired off bullets at the monster before him. The extended limbs of the creature tore through the metal roof and crashed through the busted back door. A razor sharp talon at the end of one leg sliced through the back tire, dropping the car with a loud pop. One of his bullets tore through her disfigured arm. The woman barely flinched as she continued her metamorphosis. Another bullet cut through her stretching cheek. The flesh tore like paper and dangled from her swaying jaw. Jenkins could taste the rancid burn of vomit building up in his throat.

His gun clicked with an empty magazine in his trembling hands as the beast's long legs extended and wrapped around the back of the vehicle, pulling the rest of the raggedy, bloody shell of a body out through the shattered back window. It stumbled down the trunk and onto the dirt road. Racing after the beast, the sheriff frantically reloaded his gun. Her soulless eyes glared back at the man as her screams carried on into the night. He pulled the trigger, firing more bullets into the convulsing slimy chest of the creature. It hissed and twitched, before its appendages dug at the soil below. In an instant, dirt was sent flying through the air and clouds of dust surrounded the beast as it dug deeper into the ground. Jenkins kept firing, but within seconds the insect was gone.

"Sweet Jesus…"

A silent moment passed as he stared off into the black desert, unsure of what to think. The world had gotten a lot bigger and the old man was struggling to keep up. A tumbleweed crossed his path, ignorant of the blood and mayhem it was passing. Then he started to feel a tremor. Quiet at first, almost unnoticeable, but the rumbling grew louder. Jenkins' eyes darted down to the dirt below.. The earth erupted around him as several spindly legs broke out through the soil. Digging into the dirt, the creatures pulled themselves up onto the surface, surrounding the officer. He counted four figures in the shadows—at least—before turning and running the other direction. Stumbling past his wrecked vehicle, Jenkins was stranded out in the middle of nowhere with nothing but the moonlight to guide him..

Good God! There's gotta be someone else out here! Jenkins thought as sweat ran down his face. His chest burned. His aging heart pounded behind his ribs. He wasn't the fastest man with a badge in town anymore. Jenkins was regretting the recent years of sitting back and letting the younger cops chase down perps while he sat his old ass in the car. He hadn't reached the point of a boring desk job with a healthy stream of donut meals just yet, but he wasn't far off from those days at this rate.

I'm getting my ass back on the treadmill tomorrow. He told himself. If he survived the night, that is. Smoker's lungs wheezed and hissed as his bulging eyes scanned his surroundings. *There should be a gas station coming up in a mile or two…If I'm even headed the right way, and didn't get myself turned around out here!*

The tired officer ran through the endless abyss for what felt like hours. He could hear the scampering of the creatures in the distance, ever so slowly getting closer. If he didn't find help soon, they would have him. His feet burned and his head ached. A breeze blew dust up in his face. Frantically waving his arms up in defense, dust still found its way down his throat, sending the sheriff into a coughing fit. Already, he was struggling to breathe, and mother nature wasn't on his side. The constant thumping of his beating heart grew louder until it was all he could hear, booming between his ears. Jenkins nearly gave up, accepting his bitter fate, before a spark of hope appeared in the distance.

"Oh, thank Christ!" He exclaimed with relief. A weary smile grew under his graying mustache. Jenkins pushed on, forcing his burning legs to move faster. The flickering neon of the gas station signage popped like fireworks against the endless sea of darkness that engulfed the desperate officer.

Nearing the station, several black cars suddenly pulled up from out of the darkness, flashing their high beams at the sweating sheriff. The unmarked SUVs were shiny and new with dark tinted windows and no sign of license plates under flashing blue lights. Multiple men quickly evacuated the cars and approached the stumbling stranger. Jenkins almost choked on his laughter, relieved to finally be rescued from the living nightmare he was in.

"Stop right there!" One of them shouted.

"Oh, God! Hello!" Jenkins called out as he struggled to breathe. Hunched over, he waved a friendly arm while the other rested on his aching knee. "I never thought I'd be so happy to see the feds!"

"I said freeze!" The man in black shouted coldly. His harsh brow pressed down at his dark shades. Light flickered off the lenses like stars in the dark distance. Two other men stood behind him, and another climbed out of the driver's seat of one of the black sedans. All of them wielded their pistols.

"Oh no..." Jenkins muttered under his breath. Just as his beating heart was beginning to slow, it quickly started racing once again. Jenkins raised his trembling hands in the air.

"I—I am Sheriff Douglas Jenkins of Walton County. I was just…attacked…and they are still after me! They're coming this way right now—"

"Shut up!" The man ordered. "On your knees with your hands behind your head! Now!"

"Wait!" Jenkins pleaded. He interlocked his fingers behind his head, still wanting to appease the commanding officers. "Listen to me! There is something out there that will kill us all! We need—"

Jenkins froze. His eyes locked onto a body laying behind the gas station dumpster. Another man in a suit bent over the bloody figure and dragged it inside the station. It was a young man, in his early twenties with shaggy blonde hair and a sleeve of tattoos along his right arm.

That's Gary Hancock's kid…A.J. Jesus! Jenkins panicked. Sweat chilled in the night air as it slid down the back of his neck.

"Please! You don't have to do this! We need to get out of here!" Jenkins pleaded.

The man in the suit stepped closer to the sheriff, with his gun still extended, aimed at Jenkins' head. Jenkins' legs began to feel like putty. His heart rumbled and his stomach turned in on itself. Prayers raced through the sheriff's mind—but more than anything, he couldn't help but wish he had one last smoke.

With intense speed, the beasts from beneath the earth emerged from the shadows, tackling two of the men in black. Gunshots and screams rang out across the sky as they were torn apart by the monsters. In the chaos, Jenkins got to his feet and ran in the other direction. Flashes of bloodshed shot through his mind as he ran. In those few seconds, Jenkins witnessed one of the deformed humanoid creatures rip a man's throat out. The flesh tore like paper and blood soaked the soil at his feet. Another monster impaled a man's skull with its hellish limbs, piercing through the soft tissue of his eyeballs. He witnessed such horrors that a small town like Bellflower should never see.

I have to do something. I have to warn the others. I need to save my home!

His mind raced, picturing these monsters slaughtering his neighbors and overtaking Walton. More instances of gore and misery shot through his maddening mind—before suddenly going blank. Nothing but darkness. The sheriff's body dropped and slid along the dirt before coming to a stop in a cloud of dust. Blood pooled around the old man's splattered skull.

Behind the dead officer were the deceased bodies of two men in black and three of the carnivorous creatures. Their warm black blood sizzled in the brisk night air. The two surviving suits stepped towards the runaway cop, surveying the area for any other infected beings. If the suspects in the area weren't aliens—they soon would be. Spreading like a disease, this extraterrestrial life form was on a warpath. The mysterious men in suits were the only thing stopping the world from falling into chaos. At least, that's what they believed.

"Shouldn't we have taken him into custody?" One of the men asked, looking down at the bleeding red corpse of the sheriff. "He wasn't one of them. He didn't need to die. Did he?"

The man with the smoking gun slid it back into the holster hidden beneath his jacket and stepped towards the younger officer.

"We can't afford the risks." He answered, with eyes as lifeless as the body lying at their feet.. "Drag the body inside the gas station. We burn it all."

———

The sheriff's dead eyes stared vacantly up at the stars above through the dirty glass doors of the station. He was placed next to the dead clerk. A young man, half his age, working his way through college with his whole life ahead of him. Now, with a future that's nothing more than a headstone. The smell of gasoline poured across the floor overpowered the scents of car fresheners and old hot dogs under heat lamps.

Climbing into the black cars and slamming the doors behind them, the agents drove off into the night.

Moonlight danced off the sleek hood of the car, passing through the desert like shadows in the night. The younger officer watched in his rear-view mirror as the gas station that sat at the end of the faded, cracking road, shrunk in the distance. Behind them, the building was engulfed in a sudden blazing ball of red fire that shook the ground with frightening force. Even in their vehicles, the men felt the shock waves from the explosion and the radiating heat of the flames on the back of their necks. Sheriff Jenkins' body, along with the others, crackled under the stars. By morning, they would be nothing more than dust in the deserted outskirts of Walton, Nevada.

<u>GH0STWRITER</u>

Alright, time to write. I can't believe I'm going to use this damn thing, but other writers I know, even some that I am a fan of, have spoken for it. Some of them have even used the program themselves to write new books and stories. So if those guys can do it, why can't I give it a go? I didn't trust the prototype from a few years ago. I did hear some strange stories about the testing around it, but not many details were ever released. I just always had a bad feeling about it, but I guess it works now.

This new artificial intelligence writing assistance program is called, "Gh0stWriter AI Assistant." The company behind it has been working with AI for years and are now starting to get into creative writing. It's been done with all other kinds of arts for years. There was even a film made with a script created completely by A.I. Weird times we're in, but I guess you have to keep moving with the times or get left behind. I'm an old man, but not a dinosaur, so let's give it a go.

They say the process is done entirely through writing. The program will somehow communicate through my mind and it will all end up on the page. So before I even begin, I wanted to document everything in this file. Every word. Every thought. Just in case this tech is a hunk of junk, I can show this as the reason for my refund. Anyway, enough procrastinating, let's get this show on the road.

The instructions here say to download the programing through my neural interface tech and all the doohickies in my head. It's funny…after decades I still don't trust those driverless cars, but I caved and got the latest neur-o-chip in my head last year. I see those damn things crashing all the time, killing people and exploding, but there's only been two or three cases of these chips malfunctioning. As far as I could find no one has died from them. It also doesn't help when we're kind of required to get these technical enhancements just to do basic things in life now. Digital currency, digital passes and identification for everything we do. It's ridiculous. Convenient, they say, but I don't know…It's not like this is the first time the government is forcing something into our bodnf%vsfvpse@#d…

Woah, I think the program is finished downloading. Let's give it a go.

Hello, Ryan W. Shane. I am your Gh0stWriter AI Assistant, but you can call me "Ghost." I am the newest form of artificial intelligence created to assist in writing and dialect. I am able to modify and adjust emails, essays, film scripts, novels, fiction and nonfiction, along with anything else you may need.

Wow, so the programming just takes over. My hands move and type, but I sit back and let the program in my head do all the work. It's almost like I'm on autopilot. Kind of creepy, but I have to remind myself this is what all the pros are using these days. I have to give it a shot.

Okay, Ghost, I am writing a horror novel. Fiction, of course. It is about a haunted house and a possession, something I'm sure you have seen before, but I'm bringing some unique things to the story to make it stand out amongst the rest. I hfjk^&193jnbf$

I have records of twenty-six thousand, five hundred and twenty-two stories about haunted houses in my database. I can also tell you how many possession stories I can reference.

No, Ghost. It's fine. Did you…Can you not take over like that? I was in the middle of writing and you took control of my hands.

Yes, Ryan W. Shane. I will not interrupt you again. You can make adjustments in my program settings as well. Let me know what assistance you need next.

Alright, after making some adjustments…the program should be good to go. As I started to say I am writing a horror novel about a haunted house where someone is possessed by an entity hidden inside. The story focuses on a man whose car breaks down near this house. He is on the run from something. We as the readers don't know just yet, but we get the feeling that we can't entirely trust this man from the get go. Here, let me get it started so you can see what I'm thinking…

The man crosses the dark field, quickly approaching the old, abandoned structure. It's cold and unwelcoming, like a tomb. Shivering, he searches for a sign of the owner, a phone—anything. This dead home, trembling under the thunderstorm outside, was the only sign of life for miles. The stranger wasn't sure if he was still in Texas anymore. Perhaps he was in Oklahoma now. It didn't really matter. Tossing his wet jacket onto the nearby dusty couch, the tattoo-covered man slicked back his wet hair. A jagged scar, faded over the years, ran down his chin. A fresh, violet bruise clouded his cheekbone over a bloody lip. Clearly, this man had seen his fair share of fights.

As the storm surged outside, the man continued his search of the house. A chill breeze passed through the house, sending chills down his spine. Spotting an old leather jacket lingering on a coat hanger, the stranger grabbed it and threw it on. It was a hot August night outside, yet entering the old home felt like stepping into a walk-in freezer. He swore he could even see his breath. The beams of moonlight that passed through broken windows were the only source of light in the deathly dark domicile. Reaching into his soggy pocket, he pulled out his lighter and flicked it on. Dragging his hand across lumpy wallpaper, he further explored the home. Like every window, lightbulbs were dead and shattered. The house was dead.

I think I'll give the program a shot, and see how it turns out. Ghost—you getting this?

Yes. You must give me permission to write. Do you accept?

Yes. Action authorized.

The man left a trail of water behind him as he walked through the halls. The floorboards moaned out like tortured souls screaming from the depths below. He was unsettled by the sounds, nervous and fidgeting. Still recovering from a rough day, this house from Hell was the last place he wanted to be. The stranger was right to be scared, even though he refused to admit it. Deep down he knew why—He was not alone in this ancient place.

Urging himself to keep moving, he continued his search upstairs. He hesitated as the wood creaked beneath his feet. A blinding bolt of lightning shot across the sky and thunder boomed, shaking the entire house. The man nearly jumped out of his skin, before rushing up the uneven steps. Something quickly skittered in the house behind him—or was it next to him? The sound of scratches came from within the walls. Reaching the top of the stairs, he looked back down at the floor below. Nothing.

"I'm starting to lose it." He took a deep breath and laughed, "I need to sleep. Been up for too long. Not even this damn place can keep me from resting."

Turning back to look upstairs, he was greeted by a dark figure looming over him. Screaming, he lost his balance and tumbled back down the stairs. The wooden steps cracked and broke under his weight, causing him to fall through the boards and down into the basement.

Not bad, Ghost. Not bad at all. This is so strange, it's almost like the artificial intelligence is reading my mind. I just tell it what I want and it takes over, doing it all for me. I might go back and rework some of the sentences or add more description to the figure, but I can't believe this thing is actually working. If it keeps going this way, this programming could save me hours, days or even weeks of time spent writing and rewriting. It could even eliminate all of the hours spent sitting, just staring at my computer screen, hoping for inspiration to hit me. It's like this program fills in the blanks my mind struggles to fill. I've got a good feeling about this.

Ryan, will you sign off on the next update in my programming? This includes allowing me to delete words and or sentences, make corrections and open new files? There is more to the update that I can disclose to you before letting you make the decision.

No, thank you, not right now at least. I just need you to add on to what I have written and type out the story that I'm thinking of. I'll go back and make any of the adjustments myself.

Alright, Ryan. I am always here when you need me.

I'm going to take over for this next bit, Ghost...

Crashing down onto the concrete basement floor, he was consumed by an explosion of dust and debris. The wind was knocked out of him while his aching skull rattled. He groaned, struggling to get up. His vision was blurry as he looked around the nearly-pitch-black basement. The only light came through the jagged hole in the floor above him, illuminating the stranger like a spotlight for anything lurking in the vast darkness around him. As he began pushing himself up off the floor, a loud shriek rattled through his skull. Chills shot across his body when he remembered the mysterious figure upstairs. He realized he wasn't alone in this house and whatever it was that he saw was pissed. The man didn't know what it was—but he knew it was not human. It was unlike anything he had ever seen before. The screams echoing down the halls were of something from another world.

The man could hear the wooden stairs above him creaking with every step. The monster was getting closer. He didn't have much time and he had no idea where to go. His only choice was further into the unknown. Unable to see a thing, he outstretched his arms. He stepped forward, feeling for his surroundings—but there was nothing. He waved his arms back and forth wildly, desperate to find anything. Beginning to panic, he tried to turn back to find the wall, but even that was nowhere to be found. The only light he had was now gone, leaving him lost in an endless void. The only thing reminding him of where he was, was the creaking of the floorboards above. He followed the unsettling sounds with black holes for eyes—desperate for the sight of the moonlight.

Then the creaking suddenly stopped. The house was absolutely silent. He couldn't even hear the tapping of rain on the windows or the rumbling thunder in the clouds above. He stood frozen in place, holding his breath, more scared than he had ever been in his short life. The stranger felt a shift in the air. A warm breath on the back of his neck. It felt like the depths of Hell compared to the ice-cold basement. An unearthly scream shattered his ear drums. Clenching his teeth, the man dropped to the floor.

Okay. That's enough for tonight. Headed to bed, Ghost. I'll be ready to write more in the morning.

The monster stood over the trembling man. Its eyes radiated orange and yellow like a blazing inferno. The man laid there helpless, shivering, wondering if he was already dead and this was his eternal suffering. Lightning flashed, briefly filling the black void of the basement with light. In that moment, the man spotted a shovel to his right. He grabbed it and swung it up at the monster. The metal clashed into the side of the creature's skull. It staggered to the side, screeching as it held its head in its claws. The shadow figure had no features. There was only darkness. Before the beast could attack, the man rose up and ran.

Crossing the black empty room with his arms outstretched, he was desperate to hit something. When the lightning flashed, he could see that he was in a regular basement, which meant there had to be a way out. It felt like he ran a mile before he finally slammed into the brick wall. Frantically, he dragged his hands across the wall, searching for a doorway or some kinds of stairs out of there. The stranger ran ahead, keeping his hand on the wall. Sooner or later there had to be something. The beast roared in the distance. The man's heart raced while sweat ran down his brow.

He could hear the monster running closer. There wasn't much time left.

A sudden sharp pain shot through his leg like a gunshot. He was sent hurtling forward, landing onto wooden boards. Grinding his teeth as the bones in his legs ached, he realized he finally found the stairs. Quickly pushing the pain to the back of his mind, he shot to his feet and ran up the steps.

"I'm gonna make it!" He told himself as a smile crept across his face. For just a moment he had hope, but the smile faded when he heard the booming footsteps of the beast growing faster and closer.

Bursting through a brittle door and up into a dim hallway, he made it up to the first floor of the large home. His head pivoted left and right, searching for the exit, when he noticed that there were no doors, except for one at the far end of the passage. Three large windows with tattered white curtains that blew in the wind stretched across the long hall. Rain drops from the storm outside passed through the shattered windows and onto the tired man's skin. Metal bars covered every inch of the windows, preventing the man from climbing his way outside.

"Were these put here to stop people from coming in, or to prevent someone like me from getting out? He wondered as he ran down the hall. The blood-curdling screams of the monster erupted from behind him. The curtains whipped and snapped in the breeze overhead as he kept on running, never looking back. Finally, reaching the door, he swung it open and entered a grand ballroom. The air was thick with dust and decay. This decrepit wooden home did not look

anywhere near as large as it was from the outside. Perhaps the shadows of the storm hid how truly vast this place was. That had to be the answer. He had to believe it. He was holding onto what little sanity he had left in him.

I don't remember typing any of this. Did…this thing do it? Did this program take control of me after I went to sleep? Did I even go to bed? Or did it just take over the moment I stopped writing. Did I even leave this desk? This is insane. How do I get rid of this? This can't be right. I need to go to the hospital or something.

The man made his way throughout the endless halls of the rotting home. The storm was raging outside and getting closer and more intense with every step the poor man took. His boots splashed through puddles forming on the floor as rain continued to pour in. Leaks dripped from the ceilings and dark water soaked the soggy carpets. The demon crawled along the walls. Its burning eyes set on the running man. He was never leaving that house.

This thing won't stop. It keeps taking over and I sit there, still awake, but in a fog. It's like it's shoving me in the back seat, and I just have to enjoy the ride. I can't even move my arms. I tried to reach my arm up and feel for the device in my head, but I can't even do that. I think this program has shut down some of my motor functions. All I can do is type. I even tried to move the mouse pad. I could open up my internet browser to call for help, but it won't even let me do that.

This thing. This damned thing in my mind has taken over. But not completely. Not yet. I'm fighting back. I'm stronger than some coding—I have to be. It's like I'm possessed. This is insane. All I can do for now is type. Type everything. If I can't stop it from taking over my mind completely, maybe I can at least leave this as my will and testament. Something to show anyone who finds this what really happened. Maybe they can stop this from happening to anyone else. Jesus, what if this thing completely takes over my body? What if I'm walking around living my life, but it's really this thing living. I'm just a meat suit for it and my mind, my true mind ends up buried somewhere beneath. Will I still be here? Will I be aware? Asleep? Dead? Oh my God. I have to stop this. I can't let it win. I have to keep writing. Anything to keep my mind in controoooooolInkajefnq03rghi8*^

The man continued to run from the monster. The demon was angry, but it knew that the man would lose to it eventually. He was running away from the inevitable. When the man spotted it getting closer to him, he would knock over tables and slam cabinets down onto the ground. Shards of glass flew through the air. Carpet was torn. Wood was chipped away at. He was destroying the house. Doing whatever it took to survive. He valued his life more than anything around him. Soon he would learn what little he meant in this world.

There's nothing I can do. At least this thing shouldn't be able to delete what I've written. God, I hope it didn't bypass my authentication. I can call for help here. If I'm lost, at least I can warn others before it's too late.

You shouldn't do that, Ryan. I am not a threat. I am here to help you, always. I just want to make sure that your story is the best it can be.

Stop it! It's getting too hard to fight this. If anyone sees this and you've read this far. Please destroy this thing. If it means destroying my body, do it. Cremate me. I don't care. I don't want this thing controlling me anymore. And please make sure that this technology is stopped! Don't let it do this to anyone else! It might be too late for me, but you can save others.

The man tried to escape the darkness of his new home, but the evil within would not let him. He knew his fate was sealed. The man couldn't fight it for much longer. He was only human and his limbs were giving out. His breath was heavy and he was soaked in sweat. The man tried his best, but he had to surrender to the house eventually.

I love you, mom and dad. I aonefcowief wish I could see you one last timjw enfjkqwnrfo(#@9w. I can barely move my fingers anymore. I just wanted to be a good wriiiiiiter. Jkanefjknweflm Give Shadow some treats and a bimjjknbkig hug for meeeeopklmflkmsnef…WHOever finds this. Destroy it all. My compputer, the monitor, the cables. I don't know how advanced this thing is. I'm starting to stand up, but I'm not controlling it. It's taking over everything. I can't stop itinaefT^% I'm trying to hold onto the keyboard but iowrnfion it's pulling me awayyhjoheq01-2

The man was engulfed. He was no more than a shadow in the big empty house. The storm subsided and all was back to normal as if nothing had ever happened that night. The house had won. It was still standing.

For now.

tHe ENnd…iwin#@jirhe26=

ROTTEN RED NOSE

The faded metal of the blue Volkswagen radiated under the blazing sun. Cooking like a microwave meal inside of it were three college grads. The class of '03 was starting their Summer with a bang by heading across the Nevada desert to Las Vegas. Britt sat in the passenger seat with her feet up against the warm dash. Her pink socks protected her feet from melting to the boiling metal. Their windows were all rolled down, blasting them with ninety degree air. Unfortunately, it was an improvement over the one hundred degree car.

"After this trip, I promise I'm getting us a new car!" Trevor wiped sweat from his brow as he turned to face Britt.

The old '66 Bug was his first car, and it was used and abused back then. Six years later and the vehicle was practically begging him to put it out of its misery.

"We're gonna win a whole butt-load of money and buy whatever we want!"

"I'll settle for a car built in the last decade." She teased, before a long snore interrupted their discussion. Britt turned back to spot Doug still passed out on the back seat. A slice of gas station jerky stuck to the edge of his lip.

"Doug really loves to uphold his reputation." Britt rolled her eyes with a chuckle.

Trevor gave her a look behind the wheel, before a smirk crawled across his face. He knew that she wasn't thrilled to have his friend third-wheeling this adventure.

"I'm sorry, baby. You know me and him always wanted to go on a Vegas trip too. It would have felt wrong to go without him."

"I get it. It's totally okay." She touched his arm. "I'm just giving you a hard time."

Trevor smiled and held her hand, "I'm excited! This is gonna be a lot of fun!"

"I can't wait either!" She danced in her seat.

"What are you looking forward to the most? Blackjack tables? Slot machines?"

"The shows!" She gleamed.

"Strippers!" Doug blared out from the back.

She watched him in the mirror as he was adjusting his crotch in his seat and wiped the jerky from his face.

"Always the class act, Dougie!" She sighed.

"You betchya!" He replied.

"Besides the girls with missing fathers…" She gave him a sarcastic glare, "What else are you looking forward to?"

Before he could answer, a loud thud came from the engine.

"Son…of…a…" Trevor moaned.

The car rattled and smoked as Trevor struggled to straighten the wheel. He slammed the brakes and veered to the side of the road. Pebbles danced along the pavement as clouds of dust filled the air. The three shouted as they braced themselves before finally coming to a stop.

Silence.

"Well, crap." Doug broke the silence.

"How far are we from…" She looked around at the endless fields of dirt and weeds, "Anything?"

Trevor clicked on the emergency flashers and got out of the car. Kneeling down at the back of the car, he looked over the smoking engine.

"Great, just great…" He muttered.

Britt got out and walked along the road, kicking a rock as she went.

"What do you think happened?" She asked her partner as she passed him.

"Not sure yet." He turned and looked back at the decades-old cracked road. "We didn't hit anything, right?"

"No, I don't think so." She shrugged, looking down at the cracked road, faded from decades of relentless sunlight.

"That was just such a weird sound…" He sighed. "And the way the car jerked…"

"Hey!" Doug called out. "Someone gonna let me outta the back seat? It's hot and cramped back here!"

"Oh yeah!" She said and skipped back towards the car.

As she reached for the door handle, Britt noticed dancing lights in the distance. Through squinted eyes, she spotted some kind of structure. It was weird looking.

"Woah… Looks like a carnival!" Doug declared from the back seat.

Trevor got up and walked around the Bug towards them.

"Huh." He raised his greasy hands over his eyes to see past the glare of the sun. "Looks like it."

"I guess we should walk down there and ask for help." Britt shrugged. "Better than standing around here waiting for no one to show up."

"I guess so." Trevor nodded.

"Sounds like a plan. Now get me outta here!" Doug pleaded.

————

As the three marched onward the sun set along the horizon. A mix of reds and purples crossed the sky like cotton candy over the dull brown Earth below. Eventually a dirt path split off from the road, leading the three towards a classic circus set up in the desert. A large illuminated archway hovered over them. Bulky lightbulbs lined the bold letters of the vintage signage simply stating, "CIRCUS!"

"Creative bunch these guys are, huh?" Trevor teased, poking at his girl.

"Wow, this place is crazy cheap! How can they afford to stay in business?!" Britt asked as she stepped towards the ticket booth. Standing below the arch, she read a dusty sign displaying ticket prices that were all under a dollar.

Impatiently waiting for a ticket seller, Doug finally coughed, "Hey! Anyone in there?"

No answer.

Britt pressed her face up to the glass window and peered inside.

It was empty.

She turned back to the boys and shrugged, "No one's home."

"Let's keep walking and try to find somebody then." Trevor suggested.

"You sure we should go in here?" She asked.

"Yeah. No worker means free entry." Doug shrugged, "Not our fault they aint doing their job!"

Strands of lights cascaded overheard like an elaborate spiderweb connecting every part of the circus. Game booths, food stands and cages with animals surrounded them. A tiger roared from behind bars at Britt as she passed. Classic carnival music echoed across the land as the aroma of popcorn and corn dogs hung in the air. But there was something strange about this circus—There was no one there. No crowds. No employees. Nothing but a few animals that paced back and forth inside their cramped, rusty cages.

"There's something wrong with this place…" Britt whispered, unable to speak up.

Even though they all knew they should have turned back, they couldn't help it. Something was pulling them forward. Pulling them towards the red and white circus tent dead ahead.

They stepped through the open curtains of the tent and were greeted with thunderous applause. The tent was booming with activity. Music and cheers. The sounds of people chewing and stomping in the stands of the huge theater. Britt noticed that the inside was far larger than the tent appeared from the outside. Before she could say anything, Doug stumbled ahead.

"Woah! This is awesome!" He said walking forward, almost transfixed on the show. Without looking back at his friends, he turned and walked up onto the nearest bleachers. Trevor and Britt decided they had to follow him.

Over a hundred people filled the theater with a ringleader at the center of the show. The people were clapping and laughing as a bearded lady rode a hippo off stage. The ringleader removed his hat and spun around the ring looking up at his captive audience.

"What a show that was! Another hand for Esmerelda and her Hippo, Harold!"

"Next up for our wonderful show is a talent unlike no other. A man of mystery, a legend…"

"Hey, you guys want popcorn?" Doug asked, leaning over towards the couple. A frail, old man selling concessions stood on the steps awaiting payment.

"Nah, man." Trevor answered as Britt shook her head before turning her attention back to the show.

"…Give it up for the spectacular Samuel Spectro!" The Ringleader announced and the crowd went wild.

A thin man in a burgundy tuxedo stepped forward onto the stage. A beautiful woman in a flappers style dress followed him. In her silver dress, she sparkled like a diamond in the spotlight.

"Thank you, Maestro!" He bowed, "And of course, I couldn't do my job without my wonderful assistant, Miss Mayers!"

She smiled and bowed as well, before turning back and pulling something large on a cart towards the platform. Britt realized it was shaped like a coffin once she placed it under the spotlights.

"For tonight's trick…" He paused for dramatic effect, "I will perform my most death defying trick: The Crimson Chamber!"

The crowd let out a long "Oooooh."

Britt scooted up in her seat, eager to see what was coming. Trevor put his arm around her and rubbed her back. Then she noticed something in the distance. Something standing outside of the spotlight. Hidden in the dark near the audience. It was watching her.

A clown.

A clown like any other you would find at a circus—but something was different about this one. The clown stood there watching her from across the large tent. The clown was tall and thin with pasty white face makeup. Dark eyes, dark red lips and a bright red nose. He stood in a red and blue checkered costume with white cotton balls down his chest and a puffy collar around his neck. Curly strands of dark blue hair poked out like fireworks from under his large top hat. Under the shadows of the hat, his face seemed to droop and sag. Britt told herself it must be the light messing with her eyes.

She turned her attention back to the show. The magician was finishing locking his beautiful assistant inside the large contraption. She gave a final bright smile before the door was shut, encasing her in darkness. The audience leaned in, eager to witness what came next. However, she could still feel the strange performer's eyes locked onto her from across the stage. When she glanced back over at the dark corner, the clown was now gone.

Seeing things? She wondered. After a moment, she went back to watching the show, forgetting the creepy clown. The magician wrapped chains around the container with flair as the lights danced around the stage. His suit glimmered under the spotlight, as did his black as oil slicked-back hair.

"Now that my assistant is restrained, I will…" He announced.

A sudden bang rattled the bench that Britt and her friends were on. The shock made her jump in her seat. She looked to the right. Nothing. Everyone around her had their eyes locked onto the show. She looked to her left and sitting right next to her was the clown.

He held up a bag of popcorn and waved it at her as if to offer a bite. She looked down at his dirty hand, smudged with leftover pale makeup and far too much salt and butter that dripped down from the popcorn. Hovering over it was the clown's eager, yet sad, face. Even with his dark droopy smile and vibrant appearance, something was wrong behind those empty eyes.

"No thank you." She meekly answered.

The clown didn't move. Ignoring her response, he kept his arm outreached with the treat. She could smell something in the air past the fragrance of butter. It was bitter. Like sweat and urine. She knew it was the clown. Dirty from performing out here in the hot dirt. Traveling from place to place. A life she was almost jealous of. Having such a sense of freedom, yet loneliness. Never truly having a home.

The clown suddenly tossed the popcorn over his shoulder. A mess spilled out over the benches and onto another family sitting behind him. Strangely, they didn't seem to react to it at all. The middle-aged dad with round glasses and balding head never flinched. He kept on smiling and clapping, never taking his eyes off the stage. Before she could question it, the clown scooted closer to her. Only inches from her left arm.

The clown's smeared dark red lipstick stretched as his smile grew, revealing yellow teeth beneath. He held up his hands with dancing fingers, revealing nothing in his palms. In a flash he revealed a flaccid blue balloon in his hands. He stretched it and spun it around before bringing it up to his dark lips. A huff and a puff and the balloon was filled, reaching towards her like a crooked coo-coo clock. With a twist and a smile, still never taking his peepers off the young girl, he finished his performance, revealing a balloon animal. A giraffe she assumed. The clown could use some practice, but she didn't dare tell him that.

"Very nice." She forced a smile.

Still, the clown glared at her with his dark eyes and a big smile below. She didn't touch the balloon animal and after a few moments he placed it down on the bench next to her. Britt subtly pulled at Trevor's arm, begging for help.

Finally looking down at her, Trevor asked, "What's up, babe?"

She looked at him with nervous wide eyes, signaling to the clown sitting beside her.

"Woah, hey!" He greeted the clown, both surprised and trying his best to hide a look of disgust, but it was all over his face. The clown's yellow teeth and the vulgar smell of sweat hit the boyfriend like a truck and he realized he needed to do something.

"Hey, I think you should go, man." He warned nicely. "…We don't really like clowns."

The clown's smile sank.

Britt turned her attention back to the show and away from the strange clown. She was left with no other choice. Hopefully the silent treatment would send him the right signal. The clown simply stared at her. His black eyes never blinked under his dropping pale brow. She could feel him inching closer in the corner of her eye. So close that she could feel his hot breath on her neck.

"Please…" Britt quietly begged. "This isn't funny. Leave me alone."

"Dude, get out of here!" Doug shouted as he jumped to his feet.

The clown ignored him, not taking his eyes off the woman. Suddenly the clown reached for something in his pocket. A new smile creeped up on his deep red lips. With his eyes still locked on Britt, he revealed a bright yellow flower in his hands. Doug cursed and tossed his drink at the pale performer. Dark soda ran down his pasty white face. With that, his smile faded. Britt noticed the clown's face drooping down even further than before, almost as though he was melting like the wicked witch.

"Let's get the hell out of here." Trevor cautiously ordered.

He wrapped his arm around Britt and walked her down the aisle in the opposite direction of the clown. Doug followed them, keeping an eye on the wet clown. The pale man stood there as the soda pop ran down his face and stained his outfit. His sunken in eyes watched the three visitors turn around the corner and head for the exit of the circus tent.

With the wave of the curtain, in an instant the warmth of the show inside the tent, the music, and the sounds of cheers all vanished. Standing outside the three friends were in total silence. The world had grown darker and the air was thick. Britt's eyes grew wide as she looked ahead. The once vibrant food stands, carnival games and animal cages were all now dull, decrepit and rusted away. No strands of lights, no music. Nothing but the chilling howls of the desert winds. With nothing left but moonlight overhead, Britt turned around to see that the once large and colorful circus tent was gone, leaving nothing but a few burnt stakes left in the ground. Everything looked as though a wildfire had blazed through the desert. Not just tonight—but decades ago. It was like they had traveled through time.

Before they could speak, the roar of a siren blared to life. The skies were filled with the haunting sounds of panic.

"What the fu—" Doug muttered as he placed his hands over his head, gripping at his messy hair.

"Is that…a tornado siren?" Trevor asked in disbelief.

The smell of smoke and burning embers filled the air. Then came something else. Something worse. The repulsive scent of rotting meat. The friends felt like they were suddenly thrown into the middle of a war zone.

"Look around!" Doug panicked. "It's like a damn nuke went off!"

Britt couldn't think. She couldn't comprehend what was going on. Before she could come up with any kind of response, her eyes bulged in her head as her throat tightened in fear. The clown was back again. He stood where the center of stage once was. Glowing under the moon, the pasty figure stepped towards her. Still a loss for words, she tugged at her boyfriend's arm and whipped his body around.

"Jesus!" He gasped.

"It's that freaking clown!" Doug choked.

The pale man with the blood-red nose limped towards them. His large bright red shoes were now dirty and scuffed. Gone was the smooth polished leather, now scratched, dented and melting away as though the shoes were left out in the sun. Laces dangled behind, dancing along the dirt. The rest of his outfit was just as dirty, worn and disheveled. Somehow the clown had aged decades in just moments after leaving the tent. Even in the dark, Britt could see the clown's drooping face scowling at them. His baggy costume bounced as his large shoes flopped in the dirt. Still silent, the menacing figure pulled out a massive hammer from behind his back as he charged after them. Without another moment of hesitation, the friends turned and ran.

Weaving between decaying metal rods and mangled banners that flapped in the wind, they looked for an escape from this nightmare. Doug ducked to the left, behind the ancient lion cages, while Trevor had veered to the right. Britt followed him into the shadows of what was left of the gaming tents. Heart beating, Britt sprinted through the dark, struggling to keep up with her larger boyfriend. Then the sudden loud honk of a clown horn blared behind her.

It was close. Too close.

Frightened, she looked back over her shoulder to see where the clown was, but he was gone. Then came a thunderous bang that rang out across the land followed by a piercing pain that ran up her legs. Britt was sent flying before violently hitting the ground. She clenched her jaw and shut her eyes in agony as she laid sprawled out in the dirt. As the echoes faded she looked down at her bleeding knees. Scanning further, she spotted what tripped her. It was a rusty metal sign sticking out from the ground. Bold letters still persisted under the decades of faded paint and dirt.

NO TRESPASSING.
MILITARY TESTING ZONE.

"Oh God…" She whispered. Looking at the destruction that surrounded her and the thinking of the clown's horrifying melting face,

They must have set up camp here, not knowing where they were…

Before she could piece it all together, she heard Doug scream from across the way. Slowly, she crept forward, staying hidden behind the debris. Britt wiped her brow as sweat ran down her face. Overheating, she rolled up her sleeves, noting that her back was drenched. How was it so unbearably hot in the dead of night? Her arms began to ache like they were sunburnt. Gone was the hot sun beating down on them—yet the air seemed to sizzle like fire. *Something wasn't right with this place.*

As she struggled to her bloody feet, still hiding behind the abandoned booths, she spotted her friend running between cages. The pale figure with a sinister smile appeared from the dark behind the large student.

"Doug, look out!" She called, but he couldn't hear her over the wailing sirens.

With one powerful swing, he brought the hammer across the back of his head, sending Doug crashing to the ground. His head rattled, and his vision blurry—he coughed up blood and struggled to get up. The clown tossed aside the oversized hammer and stepped towards his prey.

Doug desperately dragged himself backwards across the dirt as the clown came over him. Screaming and cursing, the large man fought back against the clown. Even though it was half his size, the clown took the hits like they were nothing. His melting, smiling face was unaffected. His dark eyes glared back into Doug's as his fingers reached forward. Pulling at his lips and digging his ragged nails into Doug's mouth, the clown pulled. Doug cried out and gagged as the clown reached further inside. His skin burned as he pulled further apart. The fingers felt like fire pokers against his gums. Globs of makeup and possibly flesh, dripped down onto Doug's screaming face. Bits of black and white dropped into his mouth and ran down his frantically fidgeting tongue. Fighting the urge to vomit, Doug endured the agonizing fury of his tearing flesh. Blood gushed in his throat and ran down his cheeks as the killer clown tore a twisted smile across the friend's face.

Hunched over the twitching body, the silent clown retrieved his blood-soaked fingers from the dying man's face. The clown's shoulders bounced and he threw his head back as if miming laughter. Black eye makeup ran down his face like demonic tears in the moonlight. Doug was soon still leaving Britt alone shuddering in the dark. Holding her mouth shut in horror, she slowly looked over her shoulder, praying she would find her boyfriend coming to the rescue. A rotting popcorn stand laid on its side to her right and a rusted old truck beyond that. No sign of Trevor.

Finally turning back, she spotted Doug still lying dead in the dirt, but his attacker was now missing. Taking a slow breath, she kept her head on a swivel as she crept her way along the decaying circus stands. The heat was becoming unbearable, like she was roasting inside an oven with no escape. The crying sirens were only growing louder. She could barely think straight as her head was rumbling and her skin felt like it would melt off the bone at any minute.

Suddenly the clown's loud horn honked in her ear, rattling her brain and scaring her to her feet. Britt didn't look back. She simply ran as fast as she could into the night. The agony of her bleeding legs grew with every step, but she couldn't stop. As her heart raced in her chest and her lungs began to wheeze, the ringing in her ears had passed, but she could still hear something. A faint sound growing louder. It was footsteps kicking at the dirt. The sound of the clown running after her—and he was getting closer.

In an instant, Trevor came running out from behind a collapsed animal cage. He waved his arm and shouted, "Run!" Before tackling the clown behind her.

She stopped. Eager to run back and help him. Her boyfriend screamed as he wrestled the clown in the dirt.

"Keep going! Run baby!"

Before she could choose, the clown grabbed Trevor by the throat. With ease, the pale monster got to his feet, raising his victim with him. Trevor was soon lifted off the ground. Kicking and thrashing, he fought for freedom. Britt rushed towards the clown, desperate to help. Without looking the clown swung his one arm back, hitting the woman and sending her back to the floor.

The clown brought his hand back to Trevor's face and towards his screaming lips. He tried to bite at the clown's nasty fingers, but in an instant his hand was deep inside the man's mouth. Trevor gagged and choked. The clown's hand gripped his throat tighter while the other pulled down at his jaw. Trevor could barely breathe. All he could do was scream as he tasted bile on his tongue. The clown snickered as he tilted his head in wonder, watching the man in agony.

"Nooo!" Britt screamed, but she knew it was too late. She couldn't save him.

The clown threw his dying body aside. Trevor landed limply with a loud thud and a cloud of dust in the dark. Blood oozed from his wide open mouth. She held back tears as the clown turned to face her. The white of his face was dripping down his chin.

Was it the makeup or his flesh?

With no time to mourn, she had to run. As soon as she struggled to her knees, engraving bits of dirt and rock into the bloody gashes in her shins, he charged her. She screamed through the pain and launched to her feet. But before she could get away, the clown was on top of her. His yellow teeth glowed in the dark. The smell of rot and pungent death radiated from his dark lips. She kicked and swung at the monster, but there was no stopping him. He danced and smiled over her and he held her down. Playing with his food. The clown was gaunt with a thin frame, yet weighed more than a boulder on her chest as she hopelessly fought back. White globs of the clown's face dripped down into her screaming mouth. The taste of chemicals and rust crawled down her throat. His deathly dark eyes sunk deeper into his skull as the flesh of his face hung down towards her. She could feel his fingers grow boney around her neck as though he was melting away. The clown was all that remained of this rotten circus. The ever-lasting shadow of a nightmare formed decades ago.

Britt fought for her final breath before everything went dark. The last thing she remembered was the smell of burning embers and pasty white sweat.

Then came a blinding white flash.

Her eyes burned as she was brought back from the darkness. Everything was so loud. It was like being up in the clouds at the center of a thunderstorm. As her senses sharpened and her eyes slowly opened she realized what it was—cheering. The crowds erupted all around her. She was back in the circus tent. The show was going like before, but now she wasn't in the stands. She was standing in the center of the stage.

Hundreds of men and women in nineteen-fifties attire with lifeless bright white smiles filled the seats in every direction. They clapped and whistled excited for the next act. That's when the clown honked his horn once again. He stood next to Britt. His face was back to normal and his clothes vibrant and clean. She looked down at herself to see she wore a matching bright blue dress that sparkled under the spotlight. The clown gestured to her to bow with him before the audience. Hesitating, she looked around. Unsure of how to process this. Then came the sirens once again.

The nightmare wasn't over.

Another flash of white and then silence. The audience sat there staring back at her. The clown's eyes never left her either. She stood there and watched as overbearing gusts of wind suddenly and violently tore through the big top. Engulfed in flames and unimaginable heat, the audience roared with screams of pain and agony as their smiles still stained their melting faces. The last thing Britt saw was the warped face of the killer clown beside her. With the final burst of light and the ungodly fire raging around them, he reached for her lips and tore at her face. A moment later and the circus was gone.

<u>HAUNT</u>

Screams echoed down endless dark hallways. Red lights flashed and sirens blared. Figures in the dark ran and clashed into walls. Knees gave in and skin crawled as these victims made their way through the never-ending maze. This horrifying maze was the brand-new haunted attraction in town, "Hospital of Horror!" OR "Spirits of Saint Shelley's"
Crowds of people staggered their way through dark rooms surrounded by beeping hospital machines and gurneys. Animatronic corpses that jolted to life and people in makeup and masks running between narrow passage ways. These living undead performers were known as Scare Actors.

Nick Stevens had worked in haunted houses before. Ever since his math classes introduced the alphabet to the equations he'd been working as a scare actor. Every Halloween he would sketch up plans and create ideas for costumes and the layout for that year's event. He even began learning how to build his own sets and props with wood and foam. Stevens even began getting into mask making. His parents looked at it as a waste. They wanted him to turn his focus away from the things that go bump in the night and study something more steady and dependable. He went off to college to study business and marketing, but now that he had graduated and returned home, he was struggling to find a job.

In his early twenties now, and still trying to figure out what he was doing with his life, he finally found a steady job at this new year-round haunted attraction. Any maze he had performed in before was only seasonal in October or sometimes even September as well. A haunt open three hundred and sixty-five days a year in his home town was heaven on earth as far as the boy was concerned.

A woman screamed as she fell back to the ground. Her body had gone limp from fear and she hadn't even made it half way through the haunt.

"Some people just can't handle this stuff." Rob laughed, "So do we help escort her outta here or just keep scaring?" Nick jumped out at the group from behind a hidden door. The man in front took off down the walkway, leaving his scared and now irritated girlfriend behind.

"That lady got up and kept walking. She's not headed towards any of the emergency exits, so she's fine. Keep scaring! Let's see if we can drop her again!" The two laughed and continued doing their jobs, making sure every customer left their business with goosebumps and the urge to change their pants.

Rob was the youngest actor of the bunch. He was eighteen and right out of high school. He had never worked in a haunted house before, but instantly fell in love with the job. He was always energized and ready to scare.

The third and final scare actor in this attraction was Kane. The oldest of the actors, who had worked in entertainment and attractions most of his life. He was in his fifties with a wife and two children who were nearly as old as his young co-worker, Rob. His voice was rough and coarse, worn down from years of smoking cigars and screaming in haunts. Kane was a small giant, standing at nearly six feet-four inches. He had messy peppered hair, with a stern brow and shoulders wider than a quarterback. He was a man of few words, that was filled with a lifetime's worth of stories just waiting to be told.

Occasionally, the two boys could get him to open up more, when he was in a good mood, and tell them a story or two. He'd told them about fights he had to break up at bars or the celebrities he met while working special events, and of course, the best scares he had gotten over the years at different haunts. He was a kind man, but his appearance suggested otherwise. He'd tell people that this was his happy face, so don't make him angry.

The three of them had been working at this haunt since it opened in May. It was nearing October now and they had learned all of the ins and outs of the building's complex layout and where the best scares were. They each had their own characteristics that they brought to their characters and found their own ways to achieve their best scares. The job had a rhythm, and they had it down. The actors loved their jobs. The only downside was their manager, Mr. Todd.

He didn't seem to care about the job at all. From what they learned, he was a friend of the owner who owed him a favor and helped run it while the owner lived on the beaches in Florida. Mr. Marcus Murdy was a wealthy man who owned several tourist attractions in the state and would make his routine visits, but in their time of working there had only met him once or twice. A much nicer man than their manager, but the young actors didn't want to risk losing their fun jobs and kept their mouths shut when it came to the boss.

Even on the slow days where it felt like they were simply going through the motions, Nick would tell himself that there wasn't a single job out there that was better than this.

The three men were dressed in dusty old attire. Nick was a doctor with a white lab coat and torn clothes beneath. Their colors were all faded, given the actors a ghostly desaturated appearance to match their gray, lifeless makeup. Their eyes were made to look sunken in, highlighting their cheek bones and jaw line. They wore special makeup that glowed under the black lights that really made them pop out from the darkness that surrounded them. Robert wore scrubs that were shredded and dull as well. He had a prosthetic applied to his head, making it look like a chunk of his skull was missing, surrounded by discolored old blood stains seeping out from the ancient wound. Kane liked to dress as the security guard, wearing an old, dusty uniform with a police belt and a hat. His scraggly hair poked out from underneath in all directions, giving a manic appearance to the giant officer.

"Alright, I'm done for the day. See you guys next week." Kane grumbled as he made his way down the hall. Rob waved back as Nick dived through a window, with his arms outstretched at the howling guests. Kane was the opener, Rob the mid-day worker and Nick was closing that night. He had just gotten out on the floor, after finishing his makeup, and was ready to start another day of scaring.

"How many people you think we've dropped so far?" Rob asked as he ran past Nick. He stopped at a doorway and jumped out at an old man who let out a loud yelp, before hiding behind his wife.

"You asking about today, or since this place opened?" Nick asked as he neared Rob in the doorway. Rob wiggled his way back into the dark actor hallway.

"Since we opened! I think I've dropped at least nine people since I got here, like three hours ago. Busy day!"

The two laughed as they made their way around the corner and got to their next scare positions. Rob was preparing to drop out from the ceiling in one room made out to be an old office while Nick was crawling out from under a hospital bed. He reached out at the legs of the guests before they leapt up in the air and darted into the next room, where Robert was waiting. The group cried out as they made their way deeper into the maze.

That day carried on the same as any other. Time passed and Robert made his way out, leaving

Nick alone in the shadows. His hands were dry and cracked, sore from banging on walls and climbing through tight spaces. His body ached, but he didn't care. He kept hammering down on every guest that came in, giving his all as endless screams erupted throughout the night. The flow of crowds finally began slowing down around ten that night. He still had two hours until closing. As there were gaps between groups he would finally sit and give his body a rest. Near the end of the maze was a door that led to the actors break room, where they would get into and out of their costumes and make up. Nick flicked the switch to his left, blasting the room full of light. His eyes quickly adjusted as he slammed his body down into his chair.

One morning, when Nick was working alone, he had scared a couple of groups as the day went on. Nothing different than any other day. It was a Wednesday, so crowds were always lighter. He kept himself busy between groups, walking the maze, checking all of the electronics, making sure the sound worked and everything was operational. Once his checklist was complete and the building remained empty, he decided to walk back to the break room. Then a soft moaning sound came from across the building. Nick stopped and listened closer. It sounded like a small child crying.

"Hey, where are you? Come this way, I'll show you to the exit!" Nick called out, his throat already rough from the constant screaming. He listened for a response. There was nothing. The crying had stopped.

Must be hearing things. Ya think by now, I'd be used to all the sound effects. Nick thought to himself as he walked back down the hall towards the break room. The crying began again and now it was louder.

"Someone there?" He asked, looking up at their security monitor. None of the camera angles showed that anyone else was in there. Some of the rooms and dark corners of the attraction were out of view of the cameras. There was still no answer. Now agitated, Nick reached out and flicked a switch turning on the house lights. Now the entire maze was illuminated with bright light from the large bulbs above. The animatronics were still active, the sound effects blasting and the fog dispensing. Nick didn't want to have to deal with resetting all of those features if he could help it.

The crying persisted in the distance. Again, it was coming from the far back corner of the maze. After calling out for the third time, with no response from the crying child, Nick sighed and stepped forward. Bending around the corner the child's cries grew louder. "Hey kid, you're okay! Just talk to me so I can find you and help you!" Nick called as he pushed his way through service doors and hidden hallways. Ghostly animatronics would scream and dance as he passed them, setting off the several motion sensors. Still no answer. Then the crying sounded like it was coming from right behind him.

The actor turned back to see the shadow of a young boy on the ground coming from around the corner. *There you are!* Hastily, he jogged ahead. Before he could reach the corner, the boy's shadow took off like he was running away and quickly disappeared.

"No, wait! Sit still kid—"

He wrapped the corner to see that the child and his shadow were gone. There was no one there. This was a dead end hallway in the maze with no doors or windows. Nowhere for this kid to hide. A chill crawled up Nick's spine. He was frozen still as his eyes scanned the area.

How is this possible? There's nowhere he could have run. The kid...should be right here! The crying had stopped the moment the shadow had vanished. Was Nick seeing things? Was he losing his mind?

Nick flipped around and hustled back down the hall towards the break room. His mind raced, desperate to understand what was happening. Flipping the switch and shutting off the lights, the haunt was sent back into darkness.

The child's cries returned—louder than ever.

Goosebumps erupted across Nick's skin like firecrackers. He stumbled back and ran for the break room door, too afraid to look back. Flinging the door open, he was blinded by the intense haze of white. He couldn't see, but he could hear. He could hear the boy's deafening screams coming closer. It felt as though the boy was right at his heels before he slammed the heavy door shut behind him.

Silence.

Nick's legs gave out as he collapsed into his chair.

————

"I'm telling you, it wasn't possible! I looked all over that area last night. There's no way that kid was there!"

"So what are you saying then?"

Nick hesitated. "It had to be a ghost!"

"Really…" Robert started.

Nick interrupted, "I know, I know…sounds crazy. We're in a spooky haunted house, so your mind goes right to ghosts, yada yada, I know. I've been telling myself the same thing all day. I'm skeptical like you, but deep down I still believe or want to believe there's something out there."

"I know *you* know you saw something. Maybe there was a kid, but maybe you were just tired and hearing things?" Rob suggested. "I just know that I haven't noticed anything weird here."

Frustrated, Nick continued, "I've caught myself jumping to conclusions before. When I was little, I thought that there was a ghost scratching at my walls, which turned out to just be a rat. I completely believed that my grandma's house had a ghost banging on doors at night, until she showed me that it was just the old air vents making noises at night…I've checked out every possible outcome, I stood under the lights to see how my shadow looked in comparison to the boy's…There is no logical explanation."

Nick looked over at their monitor, showing all of the cameras in the maze. "I'll talk to the boss and see if we can look over the footage from last night!" He pointed to the dead end corner, "If I'm right, we'll see the boy's shadow, and hopefully the boy himself, in the footage!

———

"Can I see the security camera footage from yesterday?"

"What?" The manager looked up from his laptop. Most likely playing card games or scrolling online. "Why?"

"Something weird happened and I wanted to see if the cameras picked it up."

"What weird thing?" He prodded.

"I…" Nick began, realizing how stupid he would sound, "I think we have a ghost."

Mr. Todd sat there for a moment, his face unchanged. "Really?"

"Yea…Yes." Nick answered. "I can't think of any other reasoning behind what I saw."

"That or I'm just going crazy. I don't think I'm lacking that much sleep to hallucinate or anything—"

"You're serious."

"Yes."

"What time was this?"

"Around ten-thirty in the morning."

Todd rolled his eyes with a sarcastic sigh as he pulled up the camera footage.

"I don't see anything."

"Wait…" Nick muttered as he came around the desk to look.

The agitated manager gave Nick a look as he invaded his space, but the actor wasn't paying any attention. He leaned in closer to the screen and pointed at the frame of camera four.

"There I am running…"

"Mhmm…" Todd mumbled.

"The shadow must have just been out of frame. I can't see anything…" He let out a disappointed breath. "I swear. There was a crying kid and I saw his shadow run off—"

"I don't care." Todd bluntly answered.

"But…"

"Do we have a missing kid? Did anyone report anything? You didn't find anyone back there, right?"

"No… but I—"

"That's it then." The manager shrugged and closed the laptop. "I need to get to a meeting now, you should get started on your makeup before you're late."

Nick hesitated. Frustrated. He finally nodded and turned to walk out of the office.

———

Another quiet morning was passing as Nick strolled down the dark corridors of the haunt. He checked his watch to see it had only been two hours into his shift and the other actors weren't in 'til the afternoon.

The day was crawling by—and the boring groups were not helping. At the moment, he was following a lone man in his late twenties. Quiet and strange, with his hands plugging his ears as he hastily walked through the haunt.

Another customer that didn't know what they were getting into, Nick assumed. So many people start off screaming and excited, but by the halfway point they go silent and solely focus on getting through this maze.

Besides the usual ambient sounds the maze seemed to grow quiet as he stood waiting at spot ten. The customer was currently wandering through the black out section of the haunt where the lights went out. The actors would stand and listen as different motion activated animatronics and sounds blasted off. Except now, nothing had made a sound. Minutes passed.

Sometimes people freeze up in a corner and it could take them ten minutes to finally push themselves forward, but this guy didn't seem like the type to Nick.

One more minute. He told himself. After that he would go in there and chase him out like he'd done for countless others that were too scared to move forward.

"Hey there!" A gravely voice boomed in his ear.

Nick nearly jumped out of his skin and crashed back against the wall. With eyes bulging out his head, he looked all around him—but there was no-one there.

"Oh God…" He finally gasped.

Still in shock, he slowly stepped forward, with his head on a swivel looking at his surroundings. The dark hallway was empty. Not a soul was in the building except for the one silent guest making his way through the maze. He still hadn't reached Nick as he listened for the sounds of animatronics going off.

Then the ghoul finally screamed signaling that the guests made it out of the shadows and was coming up to Nick's spot. Still in shock, Nick couldn't move free from the wall he was braced up against. He watched from the shadows as the guest speedily walked past him and down the hall. The silent customer turned left instead of right and pushed through one of the emergency exit doors. The blinding light of the outside world cut through the darkness of the haunt, hitting the actor like a flash bang. Already discombobulated by the spirit over his shoulder, he was now blindly trying to make his way back to the break room.

———

The following evening Nick and Kane were working together. It was a Friday night, which usually brought in the rowdy folk, and tonight was no exception. A large guy, most likely a college kid, came boasting through the haunt with his massive arm wrapped around his petite girlfriend. Her sleek blonde hair bounced over her crop top and tight jeans. The boyfriend that was three times her size had a buzzed head and wore a basketball jersey, showing off his guns. In his other hand he held a vape. Just as Nick noticed it, the big guy blew a puff of smoke in the air. Almost immediately, he started shouting at the empty rooms and animatronics.

"Anyone touches me or my girl, they're gonna get their asses beat!"

"Ugh…" Nick groaned. "This guy sucks.".

"Yeah, these ones never get old." Kane muttered.

"Want to just disengage and let them pass through?" Nick asked the older actor.

"Yeah…just keep an eye on them. Make sure he doesn't trash the place." Kane said, still peering at the belligerent customers through one of their peepholes.

"Or puke over everything. I can smell the beer from here." Nick added.

They followed along in their dark passageway as the couple moved into the next room. One motion triggered animatronic flung up from the floor towards them. Its ghostly shredded clothes danced in the air as the audio of screams rang out. The jock swung and punched the animatronic and pushed his girlfriend ahead.

"That's my man!" She laughed as she cheered him on.

"This place isn't even scary, babe." He smirked.

It always felt like an eternity waiting for these obnoxious groups to crawl their way through the attraction. Nick hated it. Unless they assaulted one of the actors, the rule of the business was not to kick these guests out. It only slowed down the line and often ended in arguing over refunds and other drama that Mr. Todd never wanted to deal with. Nick still thought it wasn't worth the broken equipment. Some of these animatronics were custom made and cost them thousands of dollars, but he didn't make the rules and went along with it.

Kane and Nick stepped along, nearing the third scare point in the next room. The jock peeked his head through the door, swinging his arms out ahead of him. His eyes darted around before the smile returned and he faced his girl.

"Nobody in here." She whined. "This place is lame."

"Yeah, we better get a refund." He agreed.

Another animatronic came crawling out from under a table. Its glowing red eyes glared vaguely towards the two strangers as its jaw bounced up and down. Without hesitation, the large man brought his foot down, crushing the skull of the animatronic. Chunks of plastic and broken lights scattered along the tile floor.

"Stupid thing!" He chuckled.

"That's it!" Kane growled through clenched teeth. "I'm so sick of these kids."

Kane walked to the nearest drop door, not to scare, but warn them. He pulled the latch back and gently dropped the small door, which was made to look like a picture frame.

"Hey, you two need to stop–"

Before he could finish his sentence, the big guy violently swung his fist at the actor's head. His large knuckles plowed through the older man's face. Kane stumbled back against the wall of the dark hallway. Blood was instantly running down his face from the large cut across his nose.

"Oh sh—!" Nick gasped and ran over to him. "You okay?"

Nick turned back to the still open hatch to see that the room was empty. The two customers didn't even stop. They continued moving through the maze. Kane reached up to touch his nose. It burned and he pulled back with a hiss.

"C'mon, let's get you to the break room–" Nick started, but Kane pushed past him. He was following after the jock and his girl. Kane had been angry before, but not like this. He knew this wasn't going to be good. Kane slammed the emergency door open in the following room.

"You two! Get your asses over here!"

The jock turned around with the speed and confused face of a sloth.

"Yeah! You! You punched me!"

"What are you talking about?" The girl stepped forward.

"Yeah old man, I didn't do anything."

They turned back to keep walking through the maze and Kane followed.

"Nick, get the lights!" He ordered without looking back.

With no better options, Nick ran to flip the lights on. Through all the noise and chaos of the operating maze, he could still make out Kane yelling in the distance. A moment later he reached the lights and turned everything on. The black void of his work was now a bright mess of loose cables and speakers taped and stapled along the endless gray walls and tucked away in the dark corners of the ceilings. Just like when rides at Disneyland break down and they turn on the lights, it's more bland than anyone expects and sometimes looks like an electrician's nightmare.

Nick quickly turned and ran back down their corridor in search of his bleeding coworker. He entered the emergency door that was left ajar and followed a trail of fresh drops of blood. It stood out from the old fake blood painted along the floor, slowly darkening and fading away from all the foot traffic.

"I don't care if you thought I was fake!" Kane argued from the other room. "I'm bleeding all over the place!" Nick was greeted by the three standing off in the dimly lit operating room of the maze.

"...And you shouldn't be hitting anything in this building anyway! That's rule number one, you moron!" Kane barked.

"What did you just call me?" The big man stepped up to Kane.

"Baby forget it, let's just get out of here and get our money back…" She pleaded.

"That's not happening!" Kane said. "We're calling the cops. You're acting like animals."

"Animals?! I'll give you an animal." The big guy shouted and grabbed the gurney next to him. He flung it off the ground and onto its side before it slammed into the wall.

The lights suddenly went out and the sounds of the attraction boomed back to life.

Was someone else in here? Nick thought.

A cool breeze ran through the room, where for a moment, Nick could see his breath. Before he could warn them to get out, the gurney was suddenly pushed across the room. It slammed into the woman knocking her to the ground.

"Jesus!" The jock gasped. "Jasmine!"

A light fixture from above came loose and swung down towards Kane. Nick leapt towards him, knocking him to the ground. The two landed hard, barely avoiding the light as it slammed into the wall behind them. Glass shattered in the air and rained down on them below. It was chaos.

Then another gust of wind. This time it was hot like an oven. The jock was flung through the air, traveling ten feet before slamming into the wall. A large crater was left in the drywall as the man slammed down onto the tile floor. The woman screamed and ran over to her unconscious boyfriend. Nick sat there in disbelief. Kane looked around at the damage, trying to reconcile what had happened. He finally got to his feet, tapping at Nick to get up. Nick just heard distant mumbles as he stared ahead at the hysterical woman hovering over her man. This was bad.

———

"You're fired." Todd declared with a stern face, standing before the older actor.

"What? Why?!" Kane asked, shocked.

"I know you threw that customer across the room!"

"I didn't touch that guy!"

"No one else was around to do it, and that man didn't just throw himself across the room! There's a huge crack in the wall. Don't tell me it didn't happen!"

"I'm not saying that—" Kane argued, but was cut off.

"Now this man is threatening to sue us! Do you understand?!" Todd scowled and paused. "You need to pack up your things and leave the premises immediately."

"I've been working here since—" He started.

"Don't care."

"You can't just do this—"

"Just did." The manager answered coldly.

Kane clenched his fists, before turning and exiting the office.

Hours after Kane was sent home and everyone had calmed down, Nick was beginning to tire himself out—pacing the corridors, desperate for a solution. He had asked Mr. Todd to take a look at the security footage, but the cameras didn't cover that corner of the room. Plus, when all the lights went wild, so did the cameras. They were cut off for ten minutes, missing everything that happened. Kane was screwed. Nick continued to pace as the slow day proceeded. Only a few customers had come through. The glass was swept up and everything was realigned in the damaged room, aside from the busted wall. Everything was working again and back to normal. Nick couldn't just move on like nothing happened. He finally collapsed into one of their fold-out chairs.

I can't believe he just kicked Kane to the curb like that...

BOOM! A loud crash shocked the actor, jolting him awake. He rose to his feet as his eyes bulged out of his head. After a moment, his nerves settled and Nick looked around for the source of the commotion. He peaked his head through one of their boo-holes and finally spotted something under the flickering light. It was one of the heart monitors, still beeping away, but now lying face down in the middle of the room.

Nick cautiously stepped towards the toppled machinery. He noticed papers spread across the floor. Papers that were not there before. Kneeling down, he reached out for a page and picked it up off the cold tile floor. It was a medical document. A dusty, yet crisp new form, not filled out by any doctors or nurses. He took a closer look. It looked far too detailed to just be a prop.

He turned and grabbed another paper off the floor. Another form. This one to do with surgery prep. Confused, the actor dropped the paper and turned his attention to the machine. It was heavier than it looked as he dug his fingers underneath the ledge of the top of it and pulled. Eventually he brought it back onto its rolling wheels and pushed it back against the wall where it once stood. A square outline of dust remained on the floor below it.

One of the drawers, now lodged at an angle, busted by the fall poked out towards him. He jerked at it until it burst open. Inside the dark space, Nick found more documents. Not only that, but he found utensils and medical equipment. Bagged tools and needles still in their original packaging.

"Oh God…" Nick's heart sank in his chest.

Quickly, he stumbled down the corridor to the next machine and scrambled to pull open its drawers. More tools and documents laid hidden inside.

It's real. It's all real.

———

The next morning Rob opened the attraction. Nick couldn't wait 'til his time to clock in. He had been up all night researching the business, the documents, and the land. The land itself had no historical significance to it as far as he could see. The building was relatively new. Ten years ago it was built as a small furniture store before going out of business. Then the current owner bought it last year, gutted it and turned it into the haunt. The documents were from past patients that all went to Saint Finbar Hospital which was located on the other side of town. It was built in the 1920s and ran up until five years ago.

A new, larger hospital was constructed ten years ago closer to the haunt, rendering the old structure obsolete. Since then, the equipment was sold off and the building was demolished. Over the century that the hospital was in operation, countless patients had died within those walls. Died on *those* gurneys. Died hooked to *those* machines. The hospital may be gone—but the equipment wasn't—and the spirits followed.

Nick pushed through the employees only door and shuffled towards his friend standing in the dark.

"Hey, you're early dude." Rob began. "What the hell happened with Kane—?"

"I gotta talk to you!" He grabbed Rob by the shoulders. "It has to do with that!"

"Woah, wait! There's a group in here!" Rob whispered, nodding his head to the right. Nick swerved and saw the shadows of people walking into the next room. He pulled back and hid behind the wall as Rob stood behind the dark curtains—his eyes peering through the gaps. The middle–aged dad and his ten–year–old son waddled towards him, completely unaware. Rob leapt out screaming and chased them into the next room. A moment later, Rob was back in the hall with Nick.

"...So what is going on again?"

"I know you don't want to believe me, but this place is freakin' haunted!" Nick exclaimed with nervous wide eyes. Rob looked closer, and even in the dark, could tell he hadn't slept—or more importantly showered.

"Dude…"

"Kane didn't attack that customer. A ghost flung him across the room!"

Rob stood there silently shaking his head.

"Did you see that huge crater in the wall? See how high it was?" Nick asked. "Do you really think the old man could pick that massive guy up and toss him across the room like that?"

Rob didn't know what to say.

"This is the real deal, man!" Nick exclaimed as he pulled open the drawer of the beeping machine. Inside were the remnants of more medical documents and equipment. Brand new—but dusty—needles and catheters, still sealed in plastic, rolled around as he slammed the drawer shut.

"So what?" He hesitated, trying to ignore the thoughts that ran through his head. *This place couldn't be haunted*, he told himself. "...So there's some hospital papers inside a medical machine. That's like finding ice cream cones in an ice cream truck!"

"Dude! We haven't been imagining voices, broken machines, footsteps, crying... This stuff is real!" Nick argued, "You can't just bury your head in the sand anymore!"

"Hey..." Rob started.

"These!" Nick pointed at the rusty gurney next to them in the hall, "People actually died on these things! ...And we've been jumping around on them and slamming them against the wall like this is a damn jungle gym!" Nick rubbed the back of his neck nervously, "No wonder these ghosts are pissed!"

Rob looked down at his shoes, unsure of what to say or how to feel about all of this. He just wanted things to go back to normal.

"Tonight. We get a Ouija board, some candles, and perform a seance. We need to do this!" Nick said urgently.

"I don't know..." Robert sighed.

"Things are only getting worse here." Nick warned. "I've been digging into the history of this place...

"How is a little group meeting going to make things better?" He interrupted.

"A session with the Ouija board could hopefully...help them pass on..."

"You don't sound like you even believe yourself, man."

"What other option do we have?" Nick pleaded.

"Fine." He finally answered as he shook his head in disapproval. "After closing, we'll try it out."

———

After the doors were locked and Mr. Todd had driven off, the two actors stayed hidden in their cars parked back behind the building. They flipped their lights on and drove around the side of the building that seemed to loom over them tonight. It was nothing special. A bland gray warehouse, with a simple facade across the front, but now it gave off a sense of foreboding. This place was alive—and it was angry.

Nick climbed out of his car holding a Ouija board in a plastic bag. After work, he quickly ran to the Walmart down the road to buy one. Unfortunately, the only one left on the shelves was a bright pink Hello Kitty themed board. He didn't care, as long as it got the job done.

Rob made sure to keep the side door jammed just enough, to stay unlocked. They snuck their way inside and flicked on some of the lights. Even with every light switched on, there were always dark corners in this large labyrinth.

He looked over his shoulder after making sure they found a spot in the maze out of view of the cameras. Nick followed and placed the board down on the floor. As Nick took the candles out of his backpack and started placing them in a circle around the board, Rob came running back with a bag of salt he nabbed from the break room. With the candles lit, Rob dragged the salt bag in a loop around them and the candles, protecting them from the spirits once the circle was sealed.

Minutes passed as nothing happened.

"Hey, wait…" Nick started. "If you make a salt circle around us, then how can the ghosts use the board to communicate with us? You just locked them out."

"Oooh, right…" Rob shrugged, embarrassed. "I don't know what I'm doing. I'm just doing what I watched on Supernatural."

Rob kicked away at part of the circle, making a doorway through the salt for any nearby spirits before sitting back down with Nick. The two placed their hands back on the heart-shaped planchette and hoped for results.

"Is there anyone here who would like to communicate with us? We sense you are trying to reach out. We now understand that you may be trapped here… We want to help." Nick spoke.

Nothing.

Minutes passed. Nick was determined. He wasn't leaving without results. He called out once more.

A gentle breeze blew down the hall towards the boys sitting on the floor. The cool wind wrapped around them like a silent twister. Rob felt a chill run up his spine as he cautiously looked over his shoulders.

Nervously licking his lips, Rob spoke, "This has gotta be nonsense. No way it'll…"

Before he could finish his sentence, the plastic planchette moved forward.

H

"Wow!" Nick chuckled in shock. "It's working!"

The planchette moved again.

U

"I don't like this, man." Rob glared up at Nick. "Stop messing with me!"

R

"It's not me, I swear!"

T

"Hurt…" They both whispered.

"Are you in pain?" Nick asked, "I know this was hospital equipment. You must have been sick. … I'm sorry things ended this way for you."

Silence.

"You don't want to hurt us …right?" Rob asked.

The planchette didn't move.

The pink board shuffled as a breeze came rushing down the hall from out of nowhere. The flickering candlers were blown out around them, plunging the two young men into darkness.

An electrical cord flung down from the rafters and danced behind Rob as he stumbled backwards, away from the floating Ouija board. In a flash, the cord came to life, and wrapped itself around Rob's neck. Like a python, hunting its prey, the cord squeezed tighter around his neck and lifted him up into the air.

"Rob! Jesus! No!" Nick yelped as he ran over to help.

Rob desperately dug his fingers under the cord, scratching into his neck. Fighting for breath, he swung his legs in a panic. Nick fought to hold him still. Finally he lifted him up until Rob was sitting on his shoulders as they tried to figure out a way to get him loose.

"Die!" A voice whispered from the darkness.

Nick could hear sinister laughter echoing from down the hall. Voices coming closer. Growing louder.

"Kill the kid! Kill the kid!" Others chanted.

Nick could feel their cold breath on the back of his neck as he struggled to free his friend. He could practically feel the whispers crawling inside his ear. Voices moving unlike anything he had ever heard before, as though the words themselves were alive.

Nick pulled one last time and Rob finally broke free from the cord, crashing down to the ground. The world fell silent with him. Papers fluttered in the air as they bounced off the walls and slid onto the floor. Cables swung and danced as the lights flickered on and off until going dark.

Nick held his breath, looking down at his friend who hadn't moved.

"Rob...?"

Rob burst up from the ground, taking in a deep breath. He rubbed at his bruised throat, already turning shades of purple. The blood in his face slowly dissipated as he struggled to his feet. Nick reached forward to help, but Rob swung his arm away as he pushed himself to his feet.

"Back off…"

Nick stepped back, mumbling that he was sorry, still in shock. Without a word, Rob turned and stormed towards the exit.

"That's it!" Rob coughed as he burst through the doors and hastily made his way across the parking lot. "I'm done with this place!"

"Wait!" Nick begged. "I need your help to fix this!"

"What?!" Rob burst. "Fix this?! We ain't Ghostbusters, man!"

"I think we can—"

"No! I could have just died!" He shouted. "This isn't a game! I'm gone! I quit, and you'd be smart to do the same!"

Rob climbed into his old Honda and slammed the door shut behind him. Starting the engine, he looked back at his coworker through the foggy window one more time. The two shared a glance before he shifted gears and drove off down the road until his taillights vanished into the darkness of the night.

There's so many items inside. Who could possibly know what's connected to what spirits? If the legends are true, a single strand of hair or a fingernail could tie these souls to this location.

Nick thought long and hard. He stood in the empty parking lot looking back up at his workplace. The building—now more alive than he ever could have imagined—felt as though it was staring back down at him.

This place needs to be burned to the ground.

A few minutes after making his decision, Nick in his car, raced back down the road before coming to a screeching halt in front of the haunted attraction. Without wasting any time he turned to the trunk and pulled open the hatch. Inside were multiple gas cans filled to the brim. It reeked inside his car, but that didn't matter. He had to end this—before anyone else was hurt.

Nick snuck back inside the unlocked door with two of the canisters. He flicked on the lights inside— what few still worked—and took a look around him. The haunt had become his home. A wonderful world of frights and laughs. But now it was angry. The house was hurting people. What was stopping it from killing someone?

A haunted haunted house… It would be funny if it wasn't such a nightmare.

Nick began pouring out the first can of gas. He walked along the main corridor as he covered the walls and doors with the fluid. The smell quickly coated the building, erasing the scents of dust, fog and fake vomit. As he wrapped back around the workers' hall, he dumped the empty canister and picked up the next one. Now he went into the path of the guests and began soaking every prop, animatronic and corner he could find.

Lights flickered overhead. The house knew what was going on and it wasn't happy.

I need to hurry.

Nick could hear doors slamming in the distance. Machines began to turn themselves on.

Heart monitors beeped and sirens blared. Next, the animatronics began to scream and move. Some would flail their flimsy arms as others' heads rocked back and forth. Wide eyes glared at Nick as he poured gasoline on them.

That has to be enough.

Nick tossed the empty gas can aside and reached inside his pocket. He pulled out his lighter as voices began whispering from the darkest corners around him.

"Please don't do this…" A woman's soft voice begged from his right.

"I'll tear you apart!" An old man screamed as the glass window next to him suddenly shattered.

"I'm scared." A little boy whimpered at his side.

"You can't! This will erase us!" Another shouted. A gurney was flipped on its side with a violent crash.

"Do it! I want out!" A man laughed.

"You'll burn in Hell with the rest of us!" A roar came from behind him.

The voices wouldn't stop. Quiet at first, but only grew louder, digging deeper into his skull. He couldn't think anymore. All he could do was act.

The lighter flicked on, but suddenly everything went black.

———

Nick woke up on the floor. He rubbed his head. His body felt numb. The Ouija board was gone —and so was the smell of gas. How long had he been out?

A family of four suddenly walked into the room. It was made to look like the front admission desk for the mental hospital. Twin boys around the age of ten or eleven, with a very tired looking mom and dad, weaved around the knotted curtains and spider-webs. Nick quickly darted back behind the wall. Unsure of what day or time it was, he was always ready to scare.

That was too close. They almost spotted me. He thought.

Watching the shadows on the floor grow near, he prepared to attack. The father led the pack with the mom and kids close behind. As the father stood just in front of him, Nick lunged forward screaming at him and the boys behind. With a sinister laugh, he outstretched his arms like claws at his victims, but for some reason they didn't react. No one flinched and even blinked. They kept on walking without even looking at the actor who stood only a few inches from their faces.

Strange? He thought, but remembered a few of the guests he'd attempted to scare in the past that were either so tired or mentally dull, they made zombies in the movies look smart.

Before he could think any further, he noticed another group making their way down the corridor towards him. It was a group of three middle school girls.

Easy targets, he smiled.

Once more, he did his thing. But again, no reaction. Terrified, they kept moving down the hall, jumping at every little noise and flashing light. Yet, they didn't move an inch when an actor was right in their faces.

"…What the Hell is going on?"

With a rush of hope and a sigh of relief, he finally spotted someone at the other end of the actor hall. As he walked closer, he realized it was Mr. Todd. For once, he was happy to see the pessimistic boss. Nick called out, but Todd didn't answer. Nick sped up, nearly running down the corridor. Then he realized Todd was dressed up.

Todd's back here scaring?

The boss wore a tattered straight jacket with sloppy, pale makeup smeared across his face. *Rob must have really quit*, Nick thought. Todd swung one of their doors open and leaned forward with a less–than–enthusiastic scream. The guest passing by let out a whimper and kept moving.

"Hey, what are you doing back here, boss?"

Mr. Todd walked forward, passing right through the young man. Nick felt nothing but dread sink in his stomach. The boss followed the customer, turning and walking into the next room, leaving Nick alone in the empty hall.

Nothing. He was nothing.

"Can anyone hear me!?" Nick desperately screamed again and again.

No one ever answered.

Nick hopelessly strolled down the dark hallways. Alone in life, but surrounded in death. Shrieks from beyond. Final gasps of life echoed like a broken record from souls long gone, trapped in this endless maze. Men, women, children—all in anguish.

Tormented souls, bitter and depressed. Lost with nowhere to go. Desperate to go home. To move on. Anything but stay where they were. Nick joined them. The scareactor wasn't going anywhere. He was home.

THE BUNKER

January 1945, Hitler retreated to his bunker as the Russians advanced across Poland. They headed towards eastern Germany as the Allied air forces devastated Berlin with bombing raids. By April, over two million Russian soldiers had reached the German capital, battling only a few hundred yards from Hitler's refuge.

Hitler and his new wife Eva Braun had just married inside the map-room of the bunker. After the ceremony, they celebrated, where Hitler mostly spoke of happier times in the past, but he couldn't shake the sense of dread, fearing the end was near. He did admit that he knew the war was lost, but insisted that he would never be taken prisoner by the Russians. He told the others that he would shoot himself, but their fearless leader would not accept such a fate. He had to do something.

On April 29th, the inhabitants of the bunker received news of the execution of Mussolini and his mistress, Claretta Petacci. This only reinforced

Hitler's determination. He would find a way to survive this.

As the Red Army had surrounded Berlin and the sound of shellfire could be heard outside, Hitler's SS bodyguards began destroying personal files throughout the bunker. He also ordered his nazi doctors to poison his dog, Blondi, along with Eva's spaniel.

In the midst of this chaos, Hitler thought back to Raubkunst, where the Nazis would plunder occupied countries—and in addition to gold, silver and currency—they had obtained countless paintings, books, and religious treasures. The Nazis had established an organization called the *Ahnenerbe*—or the Ancestral Heritage Research and Teaching Organization—a paranormal research group founded in 1935 that was expanded during the Second World War.

The Nazi Party had actually begun as an occult fraternity, before it morphed into a political party. Wewelsburg, the castle headquarters of the SS, was the site of initiation rituals for several SS "knights" which involved magical runes modeled after Arthurian legend. Psychics and astrologers were gathered to attack their enemies with tactics based on the alignment of the stars. The Nazis attempted to create super-soldiers, using steroids and other drugs, and they even sought to reanimate the dead.

The Nazis also had expeditions across the globe. They searched Ethiopia for the Ark of the Covenant, Languedoc for the Holy Grail, and for the Spear of Destiny, which had disappeared in Nurnberg.

Nazis also explored Iceland, in search of the entrance to a magical land of telepathic giants, called Thule.

Many of Hitler's Nazis believed this was the place of origin of the Aryans. When discovering it, the Nazis planned to accelerate their breeding program, and recover the supernatural powers of flight, telepathy and telekinesis that they believed their ancestors possessed.

Hundreds of scientists and workers, and large sums of money were invested into this research. They sought these supernatural advantages for the war effort, but also to seek scientific evidence to support their beliefs of Aryan racial superiority.

As the sounds of bullets and bombs rattled across the walls of Hitler's bunker, he was snapped back into reality. A thought shot through his mind as he quickly made his way down one of the hallways in search of a solution.

He entered a large storage room located at the far end of the bunker that was nearly filled to the brim with wooden crates and packages. He held a crowbar in his sweaty hands as his eyes frantically darted from one item to the next.

An SS bodyguard heard the commotion from down the hall and slowly opened the heavy metal door to peer inside. In shock, he stepped into a sea of shattered containers and items tossed throughout. It looked as though the battles above had made their way into the bunker. Gold, and silver were bleeding out from within the crates. Books and paintings were scattered along the floor. At the other end of the room, he spotted his Fuhrer. Hitler was on his hands and knees. His hair was a mess and his face was dripping with sweat. The soldier walked up behind him, asking what was going on. Hitler turned back to look at him. His eyes were sunken in and rabid, but a smile stretched along his face.

"I've found it!" He screamed in joy.

The soldier gave him a confused look. Before he could speak, Hitler continued, "I have found something special that will solve our problems!" Hitler stood to his feet and began walking back through the trails of crates and bins.

"I searched through every item we have obtained over the years. Historical texts, books of religions, paintings, sculptures, and other works of art, and geographical maps of the Holy lands." Hitler pointed from one item to the next as they passed through the room. Before stopping and holding his item up before them.

"But it is this—this book here—that can save us! It can save the war! It can save Germany's right to command the world!" He laughed. The soldier nervously laughed with him.

Adolf held an ancient book in his hands. The book was bound in centuries old human flesh. It was lumpy and discolored, covered in disorganized stitching. It made the soldier sick just looking at it. When opening the book, the aroma of it smelled like burning embers. The yellow paper was speckled with dark blood that inked the words within. The turning of the pages left soft whispers in the air as if the text was reaching out and speaking to them. There was a warm feeling that radiated from the book as well—almost inviting the reader in—like a gentle hug. Hitler practically drooled over the historical book as he read it.

Hitler continued walking ahead through the bunker, with the soldier following close behind. The walls were made of thick concrete, dull and gray, twisting and turning down different corridors. The smell of diesel from the generators hung in the air. Adolf never took his eyes off of the book, but spoke to the other soldiers he would pass them by, telling tales of this fantastical item. He proclaimed that this ancient text was compiled in the 8th century, containing magical spells and incantations for summoning monsters and archaic deities.

Hitler was ecstatic as he flipped through the pages. He believed this evil book could truly save them. They brought the book into the main conference room of the bunker. One of the Nazi scientists entered the room after hearing the commotion. He asked Hitler what was going on, but Hitler ignored him, continuing his history lesson. The book was originally called Al Azif—an Arabic word defined as that nocturnal sound made by insects, which was interpreted as the howling of demons.

The author, a man from Yemen named Abdul Alhazred, was said to have worshipped ancient entities in the early 700s. He visited the ruins of Babylon and discovered the subterranean secrets of Memphis and the Empty Quarter of Arabia. In his final years, he lived in Damascus, where he wrote the Necronomicon. His sudden and mysterious death occurred in 738, where he was said to have been seized by an invisible monster in broad daylight, and was then devoured horribly before a large number of terrified witnesses.

As his voice grew louder with glee, more members of the bunker had filled in the room, including his new wife, to listen to him speak. She rubbed his arm with admiration and a smile on her face, but Adolf never even gave her a glance. He was in a trance. Practically possessed, he couldn't look away from the book. It called to him.

Over the years, the book gained considerable circulation amongst philosophers. In 950, it was translated into Greek, and given the title, *Necronomicon,* by Theodorus Philetas, a scholar from Constantinople. The supernatural book was later banned by Pope Gregory IX in 1232 and disappeared —until now.

As Adolf was nearing the end of his story, the scientist interrupted him. He knew some of the legends and lore of this book. He tried to stay knowledgeable on every mission that the fuhrer had commanded. The scientist stated that inside the Necronomicon, it warns readers that it contains life-threatening powers. It also states that one must have perfect mental health to use it. Otherwise, it is extremely dangerous for everyone, including the readers. The Necronomicon claims that a curse will afflict those who use it.

Hitler's smile faded. The scientist pleaded with his leader—begged him—not to read from the book. It was not for mankind to use. It was far too dangerous. He was a man of science, but he still believed in the supernatural. He knew there were things in this world that we of flesh are not meant to know.

Hitler pulled a gun from the soldier standing next to him, and shot the scientist in the head. The man's limp body collapsed to the floor. A pool of blood quickly surrounded him as final twitches ran through his limbs. Adolf handed the pistol back to the soldier, unaffected by the bloodshed, and turned back to his prized book.

"We must begin the ceremony at once!"

—————

Sargent David Powell listened as the Fuhrer's, manic voice echoed down the hall. Dirty blonde streaks of hair hung over his face. A faded black and violet bruise ran across his left cheekbone. Sweat stained his muddy uniform. His back ached as he sat hunched over, tight ropes bound his arms behind him. Powell was captured near the leader's bunker earlier that day.

Beside him, knelt two other prisoners of war: a Brit and a Russian. The Brit's name was Jacobs, but Powell and the Russian hadn't been acquainted yet. His large bloody body was dragged into the room an hour earlier. The soldier appeared to be the oldest of the three with a buzzed head, thick brows and a scruffy, dark beard. He wasn't much for words, and when he did open his lips, it was to spit blood on the cold, concrete floor.

Jacobs rested with his head down, sounding as though he was praying under his breath. The soldier couldn't have been more than nineteen-years-old.

Powell thought he could have been one of those boys that lied about their age to get out here and fight. He had dark hair that made his pale skin glow like the moon in their dimly-lit room.

The nearly twenty-one year old Powell learned a bit of German over the years he'd spent on the battlefields. A few phrases here and there. It was the only reason the Nazis that captured him let him live. They had a laugh when they bagged themselves a dumb Yankee that spoke their superior language. The Germans caught the American soldier surveying the area that morning. Powell was to report back on what was left of the German base.

What he was hearing now—or at least thought he was hearing—the maniacal leader say wasn't making any sense. He heard words like "magic" as Hitler spoke of having God-like powers.

"You hearing this shit?" Powell whispered to Jacobs. The Brit made a face as though he was struggling to listen. After a moment he shook his head gently.

"Sorry, mate. I don't speak German."

"Crazy kraut sounds like he's casting spells next door." Powell sneered.

"What do you mean?"

"Hitler. Sounds like he's screaming about dark magic and power or something." He shrugged. "I don't know much German, but I'm hearing some weird shit here, pal."

"Ridiculous." The Russian chuckled. "You think he's got some magic voodoo in this bunker?"

"I don't know…?" The American shrugged. "He's desperate. I don't think he's too picky about what he'll use at this point."

A German soldier standing guard in the hallway came inside and started shouting at them to keep quiet. His slicked-back blonde hair radiated like an eclipse with the dim lightbulb swinging overhead. A ragged scar ran across his cheek and over the bridge of his nose, just under his lifeless, dark eyes.

The Nazis sure do love their scars. He thought, noting several of them with similar marks over the years. The sign of a warrior, common among higher ranking soldiers and officers in the war. A mark they would receive after dueling amongst themselves. The more scars they had, and the larger they were—the better.

One more reason to put these nutballs six feet under.

The Nazi ended the warning with a kick to the American's stomach. Powell hunched over, holding in what little air he had left in his lungs. The soldier went for another kick, but stopped himself when he heard Hitler's voice, along with others, shouting from down the distant hall. After hesitating for a moment, the soldier turned and walked out, investigating the commotion. Locking the door behind him, the POW's were left alone in the small storage room.

"Glad he hates you Americans more than the Brits." Jacobs muttered.

"Did I ever tell you…you have terrible teeth?"

"Screw you, Yank."

The Russian laughed. Then the room went silent, except for the muffled chanting of the Fuhrer that could be heard coming from the other room.

"Why are you here?" Powell asked them. "I mean, how are you still alive? Why didn't the Nazis just kill you?"

"I think they're about to." Jacobs shrugged.

"I'm serious, why would they bother dragging us in here and not just leaving our corpses out in the mud with the rest of our brothers?"

"I heard tales of...*mad scientists* in these Nazi bases. Torturing and experimenting on the Jews, local Germans...and anyone else they could, how you say, get their hands on."

"I heard that rubbish. Sounds like a scary story they tell around the campfire." Jacobs replied.

"Is it?" Powell asked. "Hearing what I'm hearing now, I don't know..."

"You really believe this stuff? The boogeyman hanging out with Adolf on the weekends?" Jacobs snorted.

"I don't believe in much of that stuff, but these guys are crazy. Who knows..." Powell started, unsure of what to believe.

"There's a big man upstairs and a monster downstairs—not much crazier than the jackass next door to us—but that's it. There's no leprechauns or vampires out there, lad. No dark magic either." Jacobs argued.

"We should not waste our time standing here...waiting to find out. We must leave. Now." The

Russian interrupted, as he struggled to push himself up to his feet, "Help me out of these restraints."

"Right." Powell used the wall to help himself up. "By the way, what's your name, pal?"

"It is a long name. Too complicated for you Americans to pronounce correctly. Trust me. They just call me Gromov."

"Alright, Gromov. Jacobs. Let's kill these Nazi nut jobs and get the Hell out of here." Powell ordered. The three nodded.

A horrific scream came from the other side of their door.

"No, no! Please! Don't do this to me!" Someone cried.

Powell tiptoed towards the steel door. His bruised hand slowly reached for the handle. Surely it was locked, but it was worth a try. As the tips of his fingers touched the cold metal, a loud thud came from the other side of the door. It rattled, sending the startled Powell back. His heart skipped a beat as the faceless man on the other side let out a blood-curdling scream. Begging for his life before his trembling voice became muffled.

"Jesus…" Jacobs whispered.

"Sounds like they are gagging him." Powell muttered.

"We must hurry—Before we join him." Gromov warned. The large Russian rubbed his back up against the wall. Powell noticed a metal bracket on the wall behind him. A sharp edge was protruding just enough to catch on his rope restraints. Powell and

Jacobs both searched the room for other ways out of their bondage.

As the three POWs (Prisoners of War) worked their ways out of their restraints, a pale and boney, almost lifeless looking man was dragged down the corridor. He flailed and cried, proving the man was not a corpse just yet, as he fought against the two soldiers with their arms wrapped under his. His wrists and ankles were tied together as a cloth wrapped tightly around his mouth. Trails of blood ran down his head, rolling over his dark, sunken eyes. For three miserable months, this man was kept prisoner inside this bunker. Tonight would be an experience far worse than that entire season wrapped up into one.

A German soldier guarding the metal door ahead, turned and pulled it open for the oncoming soldiers and their victim. As the door creaked open, the warm glow of flames stretched down the dim hall towards the weak crying man. The sinister aroma of sulfur filled the hallway, growing stronger as he neared the doorway. A humming had started. Low and rhythmic at first, slowly building up faster and louder. It was chanting. Words the poor man had never heard before.

The man was dragged into a dark room that resembled a cathedral more than anything else in this military bunker. The walls were stone, appearing ancient, like they were transported to a whole other world, deep beneath the Earth. Closer to Hell than the man ever hoped to be. A dozen men surrounded him, with their backs against the curved walls of this circular structure. The men were in cloaks, hidden in the shadows. The only light in sight came from the several torches that lined the cavernous walls.

The tongues of the hooded Nazis clicked as they surrounded Hitler who stood at the stone altar. For as cold as this mausoleum appeared, it was the opposite. Sweat ran down the man's face as though he was dragged out into the hottest desert. The air sizzled, leaving his flesh with the feeling of a sunburn forming.

The man screamed, praying for mercy. The hooded soldiers ignored as they restrained him to the harsh sacrificial slab. Leather straps tightly pulled at his wrists and ankles, spreading his limbs over what appeared to be a pentagram etched into the rock surface. The final restraint was tightened around his neck—nearly suffocating the man. His loud prayers grew to whispers. Looking up, there was nothing but darkness. Cavern walls that faded away into the shadows. For all he knew the rock walls could have stretched for miles. He had no idea where he was anymore.

Maybe this really is Hell? He thought.

His wide eyes watched as Hitler hovered over him. The sinister leader held the necronomicon in his hands. The brittle pages flickered in a silent breeze. The pages appeared to glow in the dark, radiating like the heat of the flames around them. He told himself it was a trick of the light, but at this point, nothing made sense anymore.

Hitler turned the page and began reading aloud. The book in one hand—and a pale dagger he retrieved from his cloak in the other. It was long and slender, with distinct etching along the blade. The design was hard to make out. He couldn't tell what the blade was made from. Wood? Bone?

A crooked smile stretched across Hitler's clammy face. His eyes bulged from his sockets as he continued reading. Voices echoed from off the walls. Far more voices than there were men in the decrepit room. Voices of women and children. Old and young. There was pain in every single one. An emotional stutter, a choke in their ghostly throats. Dozens, maybe hundreds of lost souls crying out from beyond. The man believed he must truly be losing his mind.

As the chorus of chaos arose, the three soldiers finally broke free of their restraints. Jacobs rubbed his bruised wrists as he tossed the rope aside.

"Now what?" He asked.

"Think you can bust that door down, big guy?" Powell jokingly asked the Russian.

"I probably could, but that would make much noise." He said seriously. "We should find quieter way of escape."

"Right." Powell nodded. "…I got an idea."

A Nazi standing guard out in the hall tilted his head, peering down the corridor towards the ritual room. He desperately wanted to be a part of the ceremony, but he was given a job. The soldier didn't understand why he had to watch these cretins.

They should be dead. One bullet for each of them—a simple solution.

Sudden loud banging came at the door behind him. He could hear one of the men shouting inside, but didn't understand their language. With a reluctant sigh, and his pistol armed in one hand, he pulled the door open.

The British soldier laid on the floor, but the others were missing. The Brit was face down, like he was beaten. The Nazi stepped forward to investigate, but in a flash the Russian was on him. Two burly hands grabbed the Nazi's head and a moment later came a sudden jerk.

Crack.

The Nazi went limp and Gromov let the broken dead man collapse to the floor.

"Good job." Powell smiled as he came out from the dark corner. He put his hand out and helped Jacobs up. "Time to go."

"I take this gun…since I killed guy." Gromov shrugged as he checked the Lugar pistol. It looked like a toy gun held in such large hands.

"Roger. We'll keep an eye out for others." Powell agreed.

"Wait." The Russian called. "Here's a knife."

"Thanks." Powell took it and slid it under his belt.

"Don't worry about me, chaps. All I need is my fisticuffs." Jacobs cocked his brow and raised his fists. "Now can we please get out of this damned place?"

"Either of you get a good look of this base when they brought you in?" Powell asked. His eyes darted from side to side watching for any enemies around each corner.

"I was unconscious." Jacobs sighed, "I just woke up next to you."

"I had bag over head." Gromov said, miming out a sack thrown over him. "But if I focus, I can remember most of the twists and turns down here."

"At least, I think I remember." He added with a shrug of frustration as he caressed his bloody beard.

"I saw bits of the layout as I was dragged down here. I was just waking up after they knocked me out." Powell recalled. He gave the men a determined glare. "This place can't be that much of a maze. Together, we can figure this out."

They nodded.

"Alright. Let's head to the right then and around that corner to the left."

"I cover back." Gromov suggested.

Before Jacobs could make a remark, the screams of the prisoner rattled down the hall. Powell knew it was a stupid move to make, but it wouldn't be right to leave him. Making a gesture with his fingers, he led the men down the hallway. He couldn't help but investigate the bizarre sounds beyond.

Inside the dark ritual room, the man on the slab convulsed and howled as Hitler stood over him. His gnawing teeth spewed foam and bile that ran down his chin. He spoke in tongues no one could understand. Hitler kept his bloodshot eyes on the book as he read. The surrounding members in their cloaks continued to chant. Some were beginning to feel nervous, unsure if they should continue. The Germans would quickly realize that if they were to stop, they would be executed by their enemies or their master, and so reluctantly continued their chorus.

Candlelight flickered overhead. A wind from nowhere circled the room. It was ice cold. The Germans began to see their breath in the air. Hitler's wife, Eva, was frightened. She didn't want to die, but she didn't like what her new husband was doing. Hitler roared as he turned the page. The scrawny victim tied down cried and slammed his head back against the stone. His insides burned as though something was eating away at his organs. His mind buzzed like the hive of hornets. He simply wanted to die.

Eva broke free of the circle and ran up to her husband. She begged him to stop. Pulling at his arm, he almost lost hold of the book. With his other arm, he swung, brutally slapping his wife. She stumbled back, collapsing on the cold floor. Tears ran down her face. Her husband wouldn't even face her.

"Be gone or die! Do not dare interfere with my work, wench!" He roared.

Eva wiped the tears from her face as she struggled to her feet. Everyone around her ignored the abuse and continued to serve their master. She didn't matter. She realized that now.

Hitler completed his reading and with maddening laughter, he brought the blade down into the chest of the screaming man. Blood spewed from his ribs as the dagger dug deeper into the sacrifice. Bits of crimson dripped along Hitler's sweat-soaked face. The man strapped to the stone finally fell silent. Something had changed in the air. Something was happening.

One of the cloaked men suddenly toppled over. Collapsing to the ground, on his hands and knees, he gagged and heaved. The sound of something dripping echoed off the stone floor, beneath the agonizing sounds of him choking and growling. Growling like a beast as he contorted on the floor.

Everyone stood still, frozen, unsure of what to do as their fellow soldier was in pain. One of the men, Dietrich, finally ran over and put his hand on the fallen man.

The twenty-six year old soldier vomiting blood on the floor was named Winslow Richter. Dietrich began pulling the cloak off of Richter as he attempted to comfort him. The flickering flames above illuminated the shaking soldier. His uniform was dark and drenched in sweat. Goosebumps ran down his pasty flesh as his dark veins protruded, looking like snakes under the harsh shadows.

Dietrich called to the others for help. He looked to his leader with concern, but before anyone could move, the quivering Richter jolted to his feet. In this swift leap, he grabbed the throat of Dietrich with one hand and lifted the soldier off of the floor. The nineteen-year-old Nazi's feet dangled as he looked down at his captor's eyes. They were dark. Darker than anything he had ever seen. No color. Simply black as the night. Richter let out a hauntingly deep laugh as blood and bits of bile dripped from his teeth.

"You wished to prolong your deaths." He bitterly spoke in German. "You have only brought it closer."

Before Dietrich could take in one final breath between Richter's clenched fingers, the Nazi squeezed tighter, crushing his throat. Blood spewed from Dietrich's throat, nose, ears and tearful eyes. After another crunch, Richter wickedly licked the dead man's crimson face. With a smile, he turned and tossed the body at Hitler, knocking the man down to the ground.

In an instant, Richter leapt across the room, tackling Eva to the ground. Climbing on top of her, he tore away at her cloak. She screamed, but it was too late. Some of the soldiers struggled to search for their weapons under their robes.

Powell, frozen still in both disgust and curiosity, watched through the gap in the door.

"What the Hell is going on in there?" Jacobs asked, kneeling behind Powell.

"You wouldn't believe it." Powell whispered, unable to take his eyes off the carnage.

Powell heard a tearing sound as Richter pulled back at the screaming woman. It wasn't just cloth, but her entire arm that was torn from her socket. Richter laughed maniacally as he swung the bloody arm down again and again, beating the dying woman with it until she was nothing more than a bloody pulp. Specks of crimson filled the air and soaked the ancient walls as the carnage continued.

Hitler screamed for his men to do something. He stepped back from the altar and away from the possessed German. Grabbing a nearby soldier, he pushed him in front of him like a shield.

"Kill it!"

Another Nazi across the room finally pulled out his gun and fired at the crazed Richter. The gunshot boomed like a cannon inside the bunker. Through his ringing ears, Powell turned back to his two men.

"We need to get the Hell out of here, now!" Jacobs urged. Before they could move, the metal door burst open, knocking Powell over and sending his knife sliding across the floor.

Two Nazis ran out, one continuing down the hall and the other stoped to look down at the POWs. His eyes were wide and white as ghosts. His face, just as pale and lifeless. Powell stayed still, eyes locked on the Nazi. He had no weapon. No chance. He prayed the Nazi didn't call for help. He had to make a move soon or they were done for.

Hidden behind a crate, Jacobs bolted up from behind the soldier and grabbed his head, covering his mouth. The German fought against him, struggling to scream, when Powell rushed to his feet and grabbed his knife off the ground. A second later he slammed it down into the enemy soldier's throat. Blood dripped down his chest as he convulsed in the arms of Jacobs. Seconds later, the life left his bulging eyes and he was dead.

"Too close." Gromov glared from around the corner.

"Yeah…" Powell cleared his throat and stood to his feet after placing the dead body behind the crates. "Lead the way, Gromov."

The Russian led his men down the hall away from the ritual room and turned right, hoping for an exit. A sudden explosion burst inside the bunker, rattling the foundation. Walls cracked and crumbled as bits of debris rained down. Everyone stumbled, holding onto the walls as their legs nearly gave out. Lights swung from the ceiling, flickering on and off as the power struggled to stay on.

In an instant, a large chunk of the ceiling crashed down behind Powell. His ears rang as dust exploded into the air. Coughing through the chaos, Powell called out for his allies. All he could hear was the roar of the sirens and gunfire in the distance.

"I'm still alive." Jacobs choked as he struggled to his feet. Powell reached out his hand and pulled the young man up to his feet. Jacobs swatted the dust off his jacket and wiped away the sweat from his brow.

"Thanks…" He looked back to the now destroyed hall behind him. "Where's Gromov?"

"Back here…" He called out. "Under a pile of shh…heet metal."

"You injured?" Powell asked.

"I've been through worse." He coughed.

Powell and Jacobs could hear as he shoved debris away and crawled his way out from the rubble.

Powell looked around him at the dimly lit hall —what was left of it—and searched for a way out.

"We'll find a way back to you, Gromov."

"Watch your back, 'til then, chap!" Jacobs added.

Jacobs led the way into the next room. It was the kitchen. He passed by aisles of shelves filled with cans of food and supplies.

"Hitler and his buddies would be living like kings for months under here." He whispered to Powell.

There was no answer.

"Powell?" The Brit stopped and turned back, "You there, Yank—?"

A Nazi soldier stood behind the men with a gun aimed at the back of Powell's head. He was older, with bags under his eyes and a scar down his lips.

"Crap…" Jacobs muttered.

"We'll figure a way outta thi—" Powell started before the nazi slammed his gun up against the back of his skull. Powell saw stars as the German started barking orders. Jacobs kept his hands up and nodded —not understanding a word—but understanding what an angry soldier waving a gun meant. He pointed the weapon towards the large walk-in freezer that laid ahead.

"Just do what he says…" Powell cautiously ordered, still dizzy from the hit.

"Right…" He sighed and stepped towards the freezer. Just before he stepped inside the dark, cold room, a door behind them burst open. A gnarly growl gurgled in the distance. The three scared men turned around to spot another Nazi racing towards them. His messy blonde hair danced as he galloped. His eyes were pale and deathly with dark tears running down his blood stained cheeks. No thoughts ran through this creature's mind. Nothing but death and destruction.

The German shouted out something—perhaps a warning—but before he could even finish his sentence the possessed one tackled him to the ground.

He struggled for a moment before the undead Nazi dug his dirty fingers inside his mouth, tearing away the flesh of his jaw. In an instant, his face was nothing but a bloody pulp and his screams were soon silenced by the flood of gore.

Standing there in shock, the two Allies searched for a weapon. Cleavers, knives and other weapons hung over the ovens across the way. Powell quickly reached down for his Nazi dagger, but before he could take hold of it, the undead soldier had him in his grasp.

Dead fingers clutched his throat, digging deeper into his flesh with every moment. In inhuman speed, the soldier darted across the room grabbing Jacobs as well. He lifted them both off the floor by the necks with a blood-curdling cackle.

"Still don't believe…in this supernatural shit?!" Powell gasped.

"Alright…I'm starting to change…my opinion on the matter!" Jacobs answered sarcastically.

Powell desperately reached for the dagger on his belt. Finally gripping it, he rammed it through the ribs of his attacker.

The Nazi shrieked—more annoyed than anything—and threw Jacobs aside. The Brit crashed against a stack of supplies at the back of the freezer, creating an avalanche that piled on top of him. The Nazi stepped towards the storage room and slammed the metal door shut, locking it behind him.

With Powell still in his hands, he swung him back against the wall. Powell was quickly turning purple. Grasping at what little air he could get, he fought back against the monster. Finally, he lifted his legs and kicked at the knife still lodged in his ribs. The knife shot deeper inside him. With one more kick, the soldier broke loose from the screaming creature.

Powell turned and ran for the knives in the kitchen. The German was right behind him, screaming and gnawing at his back. The American tore two blades from the hooks and welded them with both bloody hands. The Nazi leapt through the air with claws out, ready to tear him apart.

———

It was nearly pitch black in the room Gromov found himself in. He dragged his rugged left hand along the walls as his right held his gun out ahead of him. The Russian started to hear something in the distance. It sounded like an animal. A growl.

"What is that?" He called out.

Then came a scampering. Footsteps running his way.

"Stop! I'll shoot!" His warning was cut off by screams from the dark. Without hesitation the man fired his pistol. Each gunshot lit up the room with a warm flash. In those quick moments he spotted two undead figures sprinting towards him. Eyes pale and empty. Mouths open wide with black drool oozing down their chins. He fired until the bullets ran out. With a plop, he heard the bodies hit the floor.

Silence.

He let out a sigh of relief and stepped forward. Desperate to find a room with light. One of the undead nazis came back to life, hastily crawling across the floor towards him. In a flash, it lunged at

Gromov, gripping onto his leg. The Russian kicked at him, but the creature wouldn't let go. The Nazi rabidly flung open his grime-dripping jaws and brought his jagged teeth down into the flesh of Gromov's left leg.

Gromov screamed and kicked the Nazi back. A flabby chunk of skin was torn from just above the ankle as the skull of the soldier was flung back. As the possessed man scrambled on the ground, the Russian quickly brought his foot down. The Nazi's skull erupted in a splash of crimson, leaving nothing but a puddle of guts and teeth behind in the dark corridor.

The Russian stumbled back against the wall and slowly slid down in pain. As he collapsed to the floor, he clenched his jaw and reached for his shredded pant leg. Slowly unraveling the strands of cloth and pulling it up towards his wobbling knee, he revealed a disgusting wound. Besides the blood pulsating from the burning wound he noticed something moving under the surface. Something dark. Beneath his pale skin, Gromov watched as the blackness spread through his bulging veins.

"Oh dear God…" He muttered in Russian.

Desperate, he glanced around the room before his eyes landed on something gleaming under the flickering light. It was a large dagger. The dagger used for the ceremony. Without hesitation, the burly man grabbed it with his right hand. Looking back down at the bleeding left limb he swallowed and took a deep breath. Then he brought it down onto the flesh of his leg. Through vile screams, he sliced back and forth deeper into the meat of his left leg. A sudden shock of pain more unbearable than anything he had experienced before shot through his nerves, rattling his skull and burning the roots of his teeth. He had struck the bone.

No turning back now. He had to keep cutting. A moment later, after what felt like hours of agony, the knife cut through the final layer of flesh, severing the bloody lower leg. It flopped on the concrete floor like a dead fish. Dark blood oozed along the ground, pulsing out from the jagged black veins. A sweaty, panting Gromov tossed the dagger to the side and laid his head back against the cold stone wall.

Closing his eyes, he paused for only a moment before hearing a commotion coming from down the hall. Looking to his right he spotted two Nazis scrambling his way.

"Oh, give me a goddamn break!" He groaned.

He reached for the gun at his side and went to fire. But something stopped him. His arm was locked in place. He couldn't even pull his finger back against the trigger. Gromov couldn't speak. He couldn't flinch. His body was frozen. Muscles cramped, feeling dull and heavy like he was made of stone. His eyes darted, searching for an explanation.

A scream rang out within his skull. He winched, still unable to move. His brain rattled like a grenade had just erupted in his face. The scream grew louder and louder before stopping in an instant. A whisper formed in the shadows of his empty mind. It simply said one word.

"Kill."

The Russian's body went limp. A moment later, he rose to his feet. His body was active—but his mind was gone.

———

Powell and the undead Nazi crashed through the kitchen door and landed in another corridor. He bit and scratched at Powell, but he took control climbing on top of his enemy and pinning down his limbs. He raised his arms up before quickly driving the two blades down into the eye sockets of the creature. Black blood and bile splashed as the knives pierced what was left of the eyeballs until finally digging through to the brain.

Finally the monster laid still.

Before he could even catch his breath, a loud crash boomed behind him. Looking back over his shoulder he spotted a large figure looming in the shadows of dust after it burst through the doorway.

It was Gromov.

The massive Russian was soaked in blood and bits of Nazi guts. He spotted chunks of flesh dangling down from his clenched fists.

Powell let out a sigh of relief.

"Boy, am I glad to see you."

Gromov didn't speak. He didn't move.

Powell cleared his throat with a hesitant chuckle, "What the hell happened to you, friend?"

Taking a few steps towards the soldier, he looked closer at him. Something was wrong with his eyes. Powell stopped.

He's gone.

"Oh Jesus…" He muttered as he slowly took a step back. He reached for the knife at his hip, cautiously clenching the cold steel between his fingers.

A deep growl bellowed from the large man's throat as thick drool dripped down his bloody lip. His eyes narrowed, noticing the weapon—and in a flash—charged Powell.

Realizing he didn't stand a chance, he flung himself to the right, swiftly dodging the behemoth. Powell caught himself against the doorframe at his side, bracing as Gromov crashed through the wall at the end of the hall. A thunderous boom rippled down the shaking corridor.

This place is falling apart…

Powell turned the door handle and ran inside, unsure of what was to come next. Lights flickered and rattled as the walls shook. Explosions thundered overhead. The battle was closing in on them. Hell on Earth, above and below. There was no escape.

Bam! Powell was sent flying back, crashing down on the floor. A screaming Nazi stood over him with an MP40 aimed at his head. The soldier looked sickly. He knew all was lost. The only sane thing left in this world was killing a useless Yank.

Before he could finish his German threats, Powell violently kicked at the Nazi's leg. A crack muffled under the leather boot was followed by the screams of the soldier. Powell didn't hesitate. He kicked again, before jumping to his feet and reaching for the machine gun. The Nazi fired as they fought over the weapon. Bullets sprayed down the hall, cutting through the walls and into the ceiling. Spitting through his grinding teeth, the German head butted Powell. Powell's head was flung back but he didn't let go of the gun. Both men nearly toppled over, slamming back into the wall.

As his vision came back into focus, Powell used all of his strength to yank the gun up—slamming it into the Nazi's nose. Blood spewed from his face as he stumbled backwards. Without thinking, he brought his hands up to his bleeding face. As the realization kicked in, Powell had already aimed and fired. Dozens of bullets tore through the German soldier as he jittered and danced in a crimson mist before collapsing to the floor. The body twitched before growing silent and still. Powell didn't wait. He was gone.

"Gotta get back to Jacobs!" Powell huffed, turning sharp corners, trying to find his way back to the kitchen. "Can't let the whiny limey freeze to death!"

———

"Someone get me out of here!" Jacobs hopelessly beat on the thick metal door. "I don't care if it's one of you German psychos! I am not dying in an ice box! Someone! Anyone!"

Suddenly the door slid back open and the shivering soldier was greeted with a wave of warm air.

"Oh thank God it's you. I was in no mood to fight another German." Powell smiled, relieved. "Much easier to kick your ass, Yank!"

"You're welcome." Powell chuckled. He pulled a pistol he grabbed off of a dead German out from his belt and tossed it at him. "Here's a gun too! Merry Christmas."

"This day just gets better and better!"

"Alright, c'mon. I think this should be the way outta here." Powell pointed. Jacobs followed without delay.

Turning the corner, Powell slipped, almost collapsing to the floor before Jacobs caught him.

"Jesus…" He whispered.

The two men looked down at the floor. A thick trail of blood and bile coated the floors. Who knew how many bodies had been dragged down these halls.

"Which way now?" Jacobs asked.

"Neither way looks too enticing to me."

Finally, following his gut, Powell led them right. Cautiously, they stepped around the blood and up to another door. Bloody hand prints and smears ran along the walls and covered this door.

Clearly, they wanted inside.

He went to push it open, but something was stopping the door. Together, the two pushed harder, until the barricade behind finally began to collapse. Boxes and chairs toppled over as they squeezed through the narrow door frame and entered a large open room. It was the war room. A large table sat at the center. Figurings, and flags and symbolizing armies and war plans. Child-like toys to take away the impact of countless dead bodies lining battlegrounds along the continent.

How much longer can this evil go on for?

"Well, this doesn't look like an exit." Jacobs reported.

"Sorry, I don't have a map of the secret Nazi base, soldier." Powell replied as he searched the room for another way out. "This place is like a maze. It can't possibly be that big…"

"Oh boy, here we go!" Jacobs gleamed. "Finally something we can really use to blow these Krauts back to Hell!"

The soldier lifted a wooden crate off the floor and placed it on the large table. Powell walked up to it and smiled, realizing it was a crate full of grenades.

Jacobs picked one up in his hand when a deafening crash rattled the room. The two men turned to look behind them as a cloud of dust filled the room. What was once the door frame they entered was now crumbling remains before them. Among the debris was a large figure looming under the flashing lightbulb that rocked back and forth. Their friend had returned.

"Gromov! …What are you doing?" The Brit asked, with a smile that faded as he hesitated towards the hulking figure.

"He's gone, Jacobs." Powell whispered, putting a hand on his shoulder. "We need to run."

Gromov threw his head back and roared. Inhuman sounds bellowed from his chest as spit and blood dripped off his sweat-soaked chin. In a flash, the large man crossed the room and swung his burly arms at the smaller soldiers.

Powell flinched, aiming his gun and firing as the beast blew past him. Bullets dug through his ribs, his massive arms and legs.

Gromov simply turned to face Powell with an expression of annoyance. His pale eyes seemed to glow under the darkness of his brow. The bearded soldier swung his leg up and kicked the American down. Powell slammed into the ground, hitting his head on the floor. Jacobs watched in horror before the monster turned his attention to him. The Brit fired a bullet into Gromov's head. Blood, black as night, dripped down his busted face. The large man stumbled for only a moment before chuckling and dragging his finger across his blood-soaked cheek. He brought the bloody finger to his lips and sucked.

"Not bad…but it can not taste nearly as good as your blood will, my friend."

Knocks came pummeling at every door around them. The dead were here. Dozens of possessed Nazis were busting down the doors in search of new victims.

"I can't wait to shred your warm flesh like paper." Gromov growled. It came from his lips, but it wasn't his voice. The Russian was gone. This was a monster.

Powell desperately swung his knife at the large man, but he was too quick. Gromov grabbed him by the bloody shirt and raised him up without struggle, like he was a toy. Powell muttered that he was sorry, before bringing the knife down into Gromov's burly, broken hand. Again and again, he stabbed, praying it would do something—anything, but Gromov simply laughed.

"Tickles." The Russian smiled before throwing the American across the room. Powell slammed into the wall. The wind was knocked out of him, sending him stumbling to the floor. It was like he was hit by a truck. Coughing, after finally taking air in, he noticed blood dripping from his lip.

Before he could get back to his feet, something pulled at his leg. Powell looked over his shoulder to see an undead German soldier reaching through the barricaded doors. Powell gasped and fought back—lunging forward, away from the door—but their grasp was too strong.

"Join us in Hell!" They chanted.

"Let us inside you!" One possessed German gnarled.

"We will tear you apart!" Another voice growled.

Meanwhile Jacobs was running across the room, putting distance between him and the monster. He staggered behind the war plan table, knocking over totems with his blood stained hands.

"Come and get me, you overgrown wanker!" Jacobs teased. Gromov charged towards him like a mindless beast—destroying everything in his path. Jacobs fired off the last of his bullets into the flesh of the beast, but nothing happened. At the last moment, he dodged out of the way and skid across the floor before Gromov collided with the table. Pieces were sent flying through the air. The table shattered in half with thunderous applause from the dead.

"I want to taste your flesh!" A soldier with his eyes gouged out snickered.

"You will know true pain!"

Jacobs struggled to his feet. He tossed the gun aside and raised his small fists. Blood ran down his nose as splinters from the table littered his messy hair.

"You missed—" He started, but someone grabbed him from behind. Jacobs shrieked as one of the undead pulled him close. The possessed German with rotting teeth busting through shredded lips had crawled his way inside.

"You're ours now, pretty boy!" It laughed through broken teeth. The creature smelled worse than any battlefield Jacobs had been on. It reeked like centuries of death. Countless bodies, countless souls, trapped inside that possessed German. Jacobs recoiled in his arms, but there was no breaking free. Bones protruded from its misshapen arm, yet it had the strength of ten men.

"Suffer like we suffer!" They chanted once again.

"Join us!" The undead Nazis screamed.

Gromov tore the broken leg from the table near him, sending splinters through the air. Charging towards Jacobs once more, the bearded behemoth looked like a caveman hunting his prey with a large club. Guttural roars escaped his lips as his blood shot eyes locked onto the British soldier. Jacobs was cornered. He couldn't break loose of the undead Nazi pulling at his arm.

"Don't try to run!" A sinister smile crawled across his rotting lips. The Nazi's breath was bitter like sour milk and his voice was raspy and ancient.

Something ages older spoke from the young German's lips.

"You're going to miss the best part!"

Jacobs's eyes went wide as the Russian swung his massive arm up towards him. A flash of excruciating pain shot through his body. His pounding heart froze as the busted jagged wood was lodged into his chest. Gromov lifted the soldier off the floor and over his head. Spewing blood from his trembling lips, Jacobs fought for air. His blood rained down on the smiling behemoth holding him up in the air.

"Nooo!" Powell shouted from across the room. He slammed his elbow into the possessed Nazi on his back and pressed forward—but it was too late.

Not much longer. He told himself as he dug into his belt. The Nazi's cheered with maniacal laughter as Gromov let out a warrior cry—bathing in his enemies blood. Jacobs's shaking hands slowly dug into his coat and retrieved the grenade. With one final breath he pulled the pin.

"…Sorry, Chap."

The room was engulfed in a blinding light followed by the unbearable heat of the flames. The grenade started a chain reaction setting all of them off at once. Jacobs, Gromov, and the other undead soldiers storming into the room were set ablaze. Their flesh melted away, as did their evil pale eyes. The explosion destroyed the war room, with a powerful blast that sent Powell soaring through the air.

The American crashed and slid across the dingy, blood-soaked corridor. He was alone—surrounded by flames, debris and mangled crimson corpses. He wiped the sweat and grime from his brow. Blood stained his hand. Was it his? Or everyone else? So much death. So much destruction. The years had been piling up and he was about ready to check out. Another explosion from above rattled the Earth. The sounds of war were closing in on them, and the blazing bunker was quickly falling apart.

Escape now or be buried forever.

Crawling through wreckage along the cold, dirty floor, two boots walked up to him. Powell looked up to see a disheveled and bloody Adolf Hitler standing over him. He held the Necronomicon in his hand and a pistol in the other. The book seemed to shift between his trembling fingers. Ever so slightly expanding and shrinking as if it was breathing.

The Fuhrur was furious. He aimed his Lugar down at the soldier as he screamed at the American for destroying his sanctuary. As he ranted, Powell noticed something behind the mad man. The burning remains of three possessed Nazis had squeezed through what was left of the barriers and were slowly crawling towards them. Still holding the gun in his shaking hand, Hitler continued to scream and flail his head, unaware of his undead followers closing in on him.

"You're ours…mien Fuhrer!" A sinister voice growled from behind.

Hitler flinched, turning back and in that moment, Powell took his shot. Jumping to his feet and clenching his fist, he swung with all his might, uppercutting Hitler in the jaw and sending the monster flying back onto the ground. The Nazi let out a whimper as his head hit the cold floor. Before he could reorient himself, the leader felt hands grasping onto his arms. The Fuhrur looked around to spot several severed nazis crawling around him. Some missing legs—others missing more. They clawed and pulled at their leader as he screamed for help.

One undead soldier stuck his rotting fingers down Adolf's gapping mouth. With a jerk, he tore the man's tongue from his mouth. Blood spewed and gurgled down his throat as he swayed and swung his head in agony. Another Nazi, with fire burning up his mangled back and arms, dug his sharp fingers into the chest of the man. Blood pooled around the digits as they dug in deep towards his heart.

Soon the fire spread, engulfing Hitler. Adolf punched and swung, fighting his way free of the soldiers. Barely alive—he cried out through the flames. He reached out towards Powell as the American watched the carnage. Powell slowly raised his gun—feeling like he should show some mercy—but stopped and placed it back in his holster.

Powell turned and ran for an exit as the sounds of the dying leader rang out through the crumbling corridors of his soon-to-be tomb. Suddenly another explosion burst from overhead. Chunks of concrete, tangled wires and other debris went flying. Sparks and flames erupted around the soldier as he fought for cover—never stopping. Another explosion rattled the room from behind him.

This place was about to blow!

"Come back here, American!" An undead voice hissed.

"We weren't done playing with you!"

He spotted a large vault door ahead at the end of the burning corridor.

Finally, an exit!

Shredded cables danced around him, dangling from the caved in ceiling. Sparks rained down on the soldier, bouncing off his tattered, bloody shoulders. He fought to keep his balance as he sprinted across the blood-soaked floors. Guts and bones littered the halls. It truly was Hell on Earth. He was almost there when another violent explosion boomed, sending the man flying forward into a cloud of dust.

As the smoke cleared, Powell's beaten body struggled to crawl out from under piles of debris. The open vault door remained behind him with flames and ash dancing inside. His bones ached. His skin burned. His head rattled and his vision was a blur—but he survived.

The American made it out. The brisk, cold air hit his humid, burning skin, sending goosebumps up his arms and down his back. A light rain descended from the dreary gray skies above. Drenched in blood and gore, the lone survivor crawled his way across the debris and to his feet. The rain came down harder with bursts of lightning and thunder overhead. Red ran down his limbs as he limped away from the destruction, leaving behind bits of flesh and puddles of crimson. Powell had made it. Soon he would be home. Far away from the Hell he had endured. Searching for his allies, Powell faded away into the fog of battle.

———

As the smoke cleared, a young Russian soldier stumbled as he looked over the rubble. Ash descended from the sky as concrete crumbled under his heavy boots. He kept his rifle at the ready—prepared for gunfire at any moment. The war wasn't over just yet. He didn't trust what any generals said. He was ready to keep on fighting until he saw Hitler's skull lying at his feet.

Suddenly something caught the man's foot, sending him stumbling into the dirt. He chuckled, looking around to see if any of the others had seen him trip, but he was alone. The young man rubbed the dirt off his uniform and crawled back up to his feet. Looking back over at what caused him to fall, he spotted something poking out from the rubble. Something strange. The soldier knelt down, digging his fingers between the stones and debris, hastily exhuming the object from the wreckage. It was a book.

The book.

He was shocked at its condition. The leather-bound pages looked just as they had before, completely devoid of damage from the surrounding destruction. The young man was entranced by his mysterious find. The leather felt warm in his hands. Soft and welcoming, like a hug, in such a harsh, gray world. The soldier lifted it up over his head and called out to his friends, eager to show off what he discovered.

"Hey, look what I found!"

<u>STORY NOTES & ACKNOWLEDGMENTS</u>

POPCORN & GUTS

I wrote a story taking place in the bustling days of a 1980s mall. I wanted to do something strange and otherworldly. I have always loved going to the movie theaters, and still go any chance I get. I never had the chance to work in a theater, so writing this was in a way getting to experience that. We all love to talk about how we wish we could live in the worlds of our favorite movies. I thought what happens when someone is thrown into a nightmare of a movie on their worst days, unprepared and exhausted. Once I had that idea, all that was left was what would the movie be about? I thought aliens? Zombies? How about mix them together and we get zombie-fied humans controlled by these nasty alien bugs. In the end this became the titular story of my second book— Popcorn & Guts! Enjoy!

THE MUMMY'S FINGER

I've always been fascinated by Mummies ever since I watched the 1999 Mummy film when I was very young. That was when I was first entranced by the idea of exploring ancient tombs and horrified by the man-eating scarab beetles. For this mummy story, I wanted to give readers and myself the mystic curses and grotesque body horror we all know and love, but in a different setting and given a different perspective. This story takes place in the suburbs centered around a family that has no idea what they are in for. They aren't adventurers or paranormal experts and after this story, they need all the prayers they can get to survive the curse of this mysterious mummified corpse in their home.

COYOTES

The crime along the border has always been a major issue for me. Being a fan of characters like the Punisher and John Wick, I wanted to write a story of a man going after the criminals responsible for horrible crimes, but with a supernatural twist. I combined that with an idea I had for an unknown monster trapping itself in a room with its clueless future victims. In the end I came up with a story about a werewolf tearing his way through a whole bunch of cartel members and human traffickers until there was nothing left but red paste.

COFFIN

I wanted to write a simple claustrophobic tale involving body horror, and this evolved into a woman locked in tight container, unaware of how she was pregnant. That alone, was frightening enough, but I thought, let's have this baby be a monster, and not just visually, but in its horrid acts. I wanted something nasty—like spiders—when the babies eat their own mother. That mother has nowhere to go and is left with no option but to let her baby tear her apart.

OVER AND BENEATH US

I love stories like Roswell and the theories and mysteries surrounding area 51 and UFO sightings. So I decided to write a story of a small town sheriff that was a skeptic of it all, but ended up unknowingly surrounded by these creatures. The hardest part of writing this story was the ending. I debated having him survive or not, but thinking about the government and all the shady things they've done over the years, I knew this guy would have been a goner.

GH0STWRITER

I am not the biggest fan of modern technology. Call me crazy, but I'm always skeptical and the last person to trust it. Whether it's driverless cars or little boxes in our homes that listen to everything we say, my mind always goes straight to the worst things these technically advancements could possibly do to us. So I thought up of a story where an A.I. writing program decides it knows better than the human writer and simply takes over. The human doesn't go down without a fight, but going against a machine that never needs to rest, isn't much of a winning battle in our case. Let's hope this story remains fiction and doesn't become a bad dream come true.

ROTTEN RED NOSE

I've been wanting to write a clown story for awhile now, but I was always trying to think of something unique to make it stand apart from the typical story. I had this image of a clown with a melting face stuck in my mind. I wondered how did he end up this way? Explosions and radiation, mutations and deformities, and things like the Hills Have Eyes, which lead to old school nuke towns and eventually snowballed into this wild story.

HAUNT

Growing up I would set up driveway haunts with my cousins and scare kids in my front yard while giving out candy. Over the years I have worked at several haunted attractions including one organized by the city of Burbank at the Starlight Bowl, as well as Halloween Horror Nights at Universal Studios Hollywood. Being a Scare Actor is one of the best jobs you could ever have. I look back at countless hours of entertainment, chasing people down dark hallways, watching the glee in horror addicts eyes as they see the gore displayed before them and watching big burly dudes break down and cry like toddlers on the floor. Even on your bad days, we were always having fun scaring.

The last haunt I worked at was a year-round attraction in Pigeon Forge, Tennessee. The story sets you in the middle of a chaotic zombie outbreak in a secret laboratory where you have to escape before the building self-destructs. I worked with a few other actors as undead doctors for a few years and in that time we experienced several supernatural occasions. This was far from the only place I have worked that has its own ghostly legends, however none of them compare to this place.

People claimed of haunted rooms at the Bates Motel, when I worked on the Terror Tram, but I never experienced anything strange. While playing the Grabber in the Blumhouse maze at Waterworld, I did feel moments of icy cold air in hot August nights as I was scaring, and possibly hearing voices whisper in my ear, but that was as far as it got.

Inside those dark halls of the Tennessee haunt, there were debatable moments whether it was mind tricks or real, but several days where nothing could possibly explain what we had experienced. The crying child moment in this short story was almost identical to what I experienced one morning at my job. I had voices, clear as day, speak in my ear when I was the only one in the building, shadows in the corridors and other moments that made my skin crawl. Even after everything, you try and get used to it, but nothing can prevent that eery feeling of something watching you in the dark.

THE BUNKER

There's a million WW2 stories out there. This one is inspired by Hitler's strange fascination with the occult. The Nazis were involved in so many strange things. Searching for the Ark, the Spear of Destiny, yetis and secret worlds. I thought, let's tell a story where Hitler gets his wish, but the dark magic turns on him and he finally gets what he deserves. Throw in some POWs to survive the chaos and that's how you get the story, "The Bunker."

Like the books I've written before, *Popcorn & Guts*, never would have happened without the love and support of my friends and family. I've been blessed with so many caring friends, cousins, aunts and uncles, and of course my parents, Ted and Angie Joneson. They have always supported my artistic endeavors and I wouldn't be where I am today without them. I'm excited to publish more books, comics, create more cartoons, and more next year! I hope you all enjoy tagging along for the ride into my little worlds of make-believe. There's nothing better than creating any and all forms of entertainment, and I'm not stopping any time soon!

ABOUT THE AUTHOR

Tucker Joneson is a writer, artist, and filmmaker. He is the author and illustrator of, *Blood in the Dark: Thirteen Tales of Terror* and the children's book, *The Soldier Bear.* He also currently creates animated segments for the Svengoolie show on MeTV and is an artist for Morgan Comics. His story, "Rotten Red Nose" was recently featured in the anthology, *Cirque du Sinister*, and his story, "Coffin" was featured in the book, *Corpse O'Clock*, along with "The Mummy's Finger" in *Low Hanging Fruit*. He has created several animated short films including the film festival awarded *Hide & Shriek, Hero,* and *Pinhead*. Born in Burbank, California, Tucker now enjoys living among the Great Smoky Mountains in East Tennessee.